D0054155

CONSTABLE OVER THE BRIDGE

Under the watchful eye of Constable Nick, the villagers of Aidensfield continue their rustic lives deep in the North York Moors of the 1960s. Greengrass almost ruins Sergeant Craddock's accident-free statistics when a hen-house falls off his lorry, whilst Nick copes with a couple of determined lady shoplifters, a roadman whose daily sandwiches are stolen and a man with a penchant for searching dustbins for old socks! Constable Nick has to perform some very special duties – such as traffic control at a donkey's funeral. Then there is a surprise Royal visitor who poses a problem of secrecy...

CONSTABLE OVER THE BRIDGE

Constable Over The Bridge

by

Nicholas Rhea

Magna Large Print Books
Long Preston, North Yorkshire,
BD23 4ND, England.

British Library Cataloguing in Publication Data.

Rhea, Nicholas
    Constable over the bridge.

    A catalogue record of this book is
    available from the British Library

    ISBN   0-7505-1819-7

First published in Great Britain in 2001 by Robert Hale Limited

Published in Large Print 2002 by arrangement with
Robert Hale Limited

Magna Large Print is an imprint of Library Magna Books Ltd.

Printed and bound in Great Britain by
T.J. (International) Ltd., Cornwall, PL28 8RW

Chapter 1

Bridges have always been rich with symbolism due to their ability to safely connect two different places whilst avoiding unknown dangers which lurk beneath. It is not surprising they're widely used to illustrate the positive aspects of linking different cultures, religions or political beliefs.

In the case of the North Riding Constabulary, however, several bridges were used as county boundaries beyond which no constable dared venture in the pursuit of minor villains – the hot pursuit of true felons offered different prospects, however. In cases like chasing murderers, robbers and other thieves, we could cheerfully gallop into the territory of a neighbouring police force. Even so, it was woe betide those constables who trespassed across such bridges into foreign police areas without a valid reason! It followed that most of us regarded the officers of other police forces with something approaching suspicion, for their presence on our patch might be construed as some kind of invasion, trespass or threat. They might even be spies, intent on stealing our ideas and innovations! Bridges were therefore very conveniently placed to serve as divisional boundaries, sub-divisional boundaries, sectional boundaries and, in the case of places like Aidensfield, the boundaries of rural beats. Their purpose seemed to be to contain things, rather than permit the exchange of ideas, personnel and police officers.

Examples of county boundaries included the bridge between Malton and Norton – it marked the boundary between the North and East Ridings of Yorkshire; the middle of the bridge at Boroughbridge separated us from the West Riding while others along the River Tees and its tributaries maintained a tolerable distance between ourselves and County Durham or the borough force of Middlesbrough. There is no doubt they helped to make us feel secure from the unwelcome attentions of invaders from those forces, even if some of those bridges merely spanned ditches or minor roads.

As a consequence, however, we tended to regard bridges which led out of the North Riding as places to avoid – it was rather like walking the plank. Most certainly, they served as some kind of invisible barrier – and not only to police officers. They contained the county dwellers and it was amazing how many rarely ventured out of their own part of the world on day-trips, shopping expeditions or other excursions. Country folk on both sides of a county boundary tended to support those market towns and shopping centres within their own special territory.

There is no doubt our well-placed bridges helped to maintain our self-contained world, rather like the drawbridge of a castle, particularly as our constabulary had no wish for reactionary ideas to be thrust upon it from the Police Department of the Home Office or other foreign parts. So far as our county bridges were concerned, therefore, we believed their presence meant a lot for which we should be thankful.

Because it was the rivers themselves which often formed the actual boundaries there was ample scope for avoiding messy and troublesome duties such as those involving the drowned remains of people or cattle, floating rubbish like three-piece suites, or even old cars and empty wardrobes. By pushing unwanted floating objects to the other side of the river, they became the responsibility of another police force. The snag was that enterprising officers from those other forces would surreptitiously float the problem back to our river-bank, invariably with the aid of a long pole under cover of darkness. If any such object or corpse was found by a man walking his dog next morning (and people walking dogs are prone to finding unpleasant things) and if that man reported the matter to us, then of course, we had to deal with it. The finder's intervention removed any scope for us to shove it yet again to the opposing bank.

In the cases of traffic accidents on such bridges, they usually contrived to happen in places which were distinctly one side or the other. There was always the question, however, about which police force would and should deal with an accident which happened precisely in the centre. And suppose an offence occurred at the very centre of a county boundary bridge – which petty sessional court would deal with it? Or suppose a person committed suicide by leaping off the centre-most point? Who would deal with the matter if the casualty died in the very centre of the river – and worse still, if a murder was committed in the exact centre of such a bridge, whose statistics would be sullied by such a crime? And which force would be left with an unsolved murder on their books if the killer was never found?

It must be said, however, that common sense prevailed most of the time. If a constable was called to an incident which was perilously close to a boundary – or even a few feet at the 'wrong' side, it was usually possible, by careful wording of the subsequent report, to make it appear the incident had happened well within one's own acceptable limits, or well beyond them if it entailed some kind of embarrassing or disagreeable problem. For all kinds of reasons, therefore, we were always acutely aware of all our boundaries, especially if we embarked upon mobile duties which carried us dangerously close to alien territory.

I had a satisfying example when I became the driver of the divisional GP car. This was an occasional duty. Those in command of our division had developed the notion that, in a society in which both the public and the villains were becoming increasingly mobile, it would be sensible for patrolling police officers to match those developments. As a consequence, divisional headquarters hit upon the idea of using a car which patrolled the entire division, especially during the night-time hours. Like criminals and tourists, it would transcend all sectional and sub-divisional boundaries but not county boundaries. The driver would be a roving police officer with wide responsibilities and he would serve a greater area in which he could be diverted to any incident, large or small. Over and above the existing patrols, he would be available for immediate dispatch anywhere in the division.

The car became known as the General Purpose vehicle, GP for short, and it was a spacious Ford Consul estate car which could carry four, or even five adult passengers at a squeeze, in addition to a wide range of equipment.

Its purpose was to cope with any incident, large or small, ranging from the rescue of cats marooned up trees to fatal road traffic accidents via administering first aid in the home, coping with offenders of every kind, keeping public order and even searching for lost ramblers. Sporting bright new livery and a rotating blue light, it was fitted with radio and carried sufficient official forms and paperwork to serve a medium-sized police station. Its drivers were selected on a rota system from the division's complement

of suitably trained constables, myself included. This meant each of us would take
our turn as the GP driver once every couple
of months or so. We would work eight-hour
shifts at the wheel and it is fair to say that it
offered both a challenge and a change from
our routine duties. During the winter
especially, it provided a welcome opportunity to work a full and varied eight-hour
shift in warmth and comfort – and no
plodding of the streets with rain running
down our necks or snow soaking into our
boots.

After a long, hot and very dry summer,
therefore, my turn to be the GP driver came
on the last day of September, normally a
warm and colourful month but in this case
marked with dense fogs, chilly nights and
heavy rain. For September, those conditions
were somewhat abnormal. I was to work a
late shift, i.e. 2 p.m. until 10 p.m., and I
must say I welcomed the chance to enjoy a
long, comfortable drive around the division's most beautiful countryside and
through its most picturesque and charming
villages, notwithstanding that this tour
would be in fog-enshrouded darkness. I had
to collect the car from Ashfordly Police
Station where it would be waiting with a full

tank along with details of any specific duties which would require my attention.

Had it been a Saturday, for example, there might have been a dance hall to supervise or pubs to check, but this was a Sunday night when, under normal circumstances, things tended to be quiet. This was especially the situation at the end of the tourist season and so, when I collected the car I checked my docket and found there were no specific tasks to occupy me. I decided that a leisurely tour, with frequent halts for foot patrols around the market-town centres, some general enquiries into unsolved crimes, a spot of crime prevention and supervision of licensed premises would all usefully occupy me until completion of my shift.

But Sergeant Craddock had other ideas.

'Ah, PC Rhea.' He came out of his office when he heard my arrival. 'Just the fellow.'

'Sergeant?' I knew, from the expression on his face and the tone of his voice, that he had some kind of task for me.

'The superintendent has just been speaking to me,' he smiled. 'On the phone, from his office. He has pointed out a singularly odd and very remarkable situation, PC Rhea.'

'Odd, Sergeant?'

'Yes, distinctly odd. Today is the last day of the current quarter, as I am sure you have realized, September the thirtieth.'

'When our quarterly returns have to be submitted?' I said, wondering if there was some urgency. Normally, we had ten days to submit material, such as lists of our official visits to licensed premises, the checking of livestock registers and so forth.

'Right, PC Rhea. And do you realize that, for the first time in memory, this division has not suffered a reportable road traffic accident of any kind during this quarter? Now, that is remarkable by any standards, but more so having regard to the fact that it embraces the tourist season, that we have several main roads running through the division and that motor traffic has increased substantially in recent years.

'No minor bumps? Dogs run over? Hit-and-runs?'

'Nothing, PC Rhea. Absolutely nothing. Now isn't that astonishing?'

'This lousy weather must be keeping people off the roads,' I laughed. 'But you'd think there would have been some kind of accident, Sergeant, in the last three months, somewhere in this division. I know we don't

15

get told about every minor bump, but we do cover a very large rural area. You'd think someone, somewhere in our division, must have had a traffic accident during that time.'

'Exactly; which makes the situation quite remarkable. The point is that none has been reported to us. It was the Accident Statistics Department at headquarters who pointed it out. As you know, they keep tabs on such things; they maintain day-to-day records and they rang the super this morning, just to acquaint him with the amazing situation.'

'But the quarter isn't over yet, Sergeant.' I felt I had to comment upon this minor point. 'There's the rest of the day to get through, without an accident.'

'You are alert, PC Rhea, as one would expect. And that is why the superintendent has telephoned every section sergeant. He is very anxious that we sustain this situation, that no accidents are reported today – there's only hours to go before we can publicize this. It seems the chief constable himself wants to praise the Accident Prevention Department, all road safety officers and uniform patrols for the part they've played in reducing the number of traffic accidents.'

'A nice public relations exercise?' I smiled.

'Absolutely, PC Rhea; he hopes the Press will comment favourably on this remarkable circumstance. He doubts whether any police force throughout this country can make such a claim. And this is where you enter the story.'

'Me?'

'As you can see, the weather is not very conducive to accident prevention, all this fog, rain and so forth, but he wants you to patrol those places where accidents most frequently happen. He wants you to show a high-profile police presence during your patrol, as a deterrent to bad driving but also to increase an awareness of road safety. All we want is for the next ten hours to pass without a traffic accident in this division. He believes that if we maintain a visible police presence in areas of high risk, we can keep our record clean – for today certainly and even for the foreseeable future.'

'And every patrolling constable has been alerted to this?'

'Indeed they have. PC Ventress is on patrol in Ashfordly this afternoon and he will be paying close attention to areas of high risk in the town. There are other officers on duty throughout the division doing likewise, so your roving duty is very important – you will be patrolling throughout the entire division, PC Rhea, which means you should pay attention to the main roads, town centres and all other places where accidents are prone to occur. The superintendent has specifically asked that you be given this advice and that you do your best to ensure that our division achieves this most remarkable record. There's less than half a day to go! This is one for the history books, you realize.'

'Well, yes, of course, I'll do my best, Sergeant, but it's not going to be easy, preventing accidents across such a huge area with just one car, especially in this fog.'

'I know you will uphold the honour of Ashfordly Section as you go about your duties today, PC Rhea. We are depending on you!' and with that, he turned on his heel, lifted his head into the air and marched into his office.

As I lifted the car keys from their hook, I did feel it would be pleasurable and satisfying to become part of a rather unique record, and although our Accident Prevention Department and road safety officers did a wonderful job, I couldn't help feeling that there was an element of good fortune in this curious achievement. As instructed,

18

however, I would patrol those areas most prone to road traffic accidents and I would make sure my GP car, in all its distinctive livery, acted as a highly visible deterrent to bad driving.

But I hadn't bargained for Claude Jeremiah Greengrass.

As I went about my tour of duty, I paid close attention to those places where accidents were likely to happen – like all police areas, we had our black-spots where, for a combination of reasons, traffic accidents occurred with bewildering regularity. They included crossroads, junctions, hills, corners, town centres, housing estates and areas near schools and factories, and so I drove around as many of these places as I could accommodate within my shift.

There was no doubt the presence of a high-profile police vehicle had a salutary impact and, as my tour progressed with no accidents reported in spite of the weather, I found myself growing quite excited at the prospect of having a part, however minor, in such a remarkable record. With my tour drawing to a close and with no reports of accidents, I began to feel very happy, but there was always the knowledge that something could go wrong in the final hour or so.

If anything was likely to go wrong, it was the perverse nature of things that it would do so during the last few moments. I appreciated, of course, that because my shift ended at 10 p.m., it meant there were still a further two hours to pass before the day ended. But those two hours between 10 p.m. and midnight were not my immediate concern and almost before I realized it, the time had reached 9.30 p.m. I was close to the county boundary, with the River Derwent separating the North Riding of Yorkshire from the East Riding, but I was capable of comfortably reaching Ashfordly well before the end of my shift. Much of the fog had lifted and there was ample time to head back to Ashfordly police station, refill the petrol tank, complete my paperwork and be ready to hand over the car to my successor at 10 p.m.

Perhaps, at this stage, I should mention that the bridge between Malton and Norton is not the only one which spans the River Derwent and separates the two Ridings. There are others, most of which serve minor, unclassified roads with several on what are little more than farm tracks. As I prepared to drive back to base, therefore, I felt sure I had successfully completed my tour and began my final half-hour with a small glow of self satisfaction. Then the radio burbled into life.

'Delta Papa One, are you receiving? Over.' It was Divisional Control calling.

I responded with some apprehension, wondering what was going to detain me as my shift drew to a close. As Control continued, I experienced a sinking feeling in my stomach because the anonymous voice said, 'Report of RTA, damage only, no injuries. Thorburn Bridge. Please attend. Over.'

'Message received, will co. Delta Papa out.'

With more than a hint of sadness that our unique record now seemed in tatters, I turned the car around in the first convenient gateway and raced away to deal with the accident. Patches of fog remained in places. Thorburn Bridge was along a minor road leading off the A170. The road ran through the hamlet of Thorburn, crossed the county boundary and eventually joined the A64 as it passed through the East Riding. There was a pub – the Salmon – at the East Riding side of the bridge, but that was beyond our jurisdiction. Perhaps a patron had raised the alarm. But even as I raced towards the scene, I did wonder if the accident was in the North Riding or the East Riding, then reckoned it must be within our county, otherwise Control would not have dispatched me to the scene.

As I approached the area, however, I found myself driving into more fog – it seemed to persist in lying low along the route of the river and, of course, the darkness also hindered my driving. It was no longer a pleasant trip and I had to take care not to become another statistic in our accident figures. As I cruised through the fog, I encountered the occasional clear patch in which I could see the tops of trees and telegraph poles, but for most of the drive it was so thick at road level that it obliterated the verges and concealed any road markings or signs that might have been present. I was not familiar with this stretch of road because it was several miles off my own beat but in time I did arrive safely at Thorburn Bridge. Even before I parked, I was aware of headlights blazing from a stationary vehicle on the verge of the approach road and a handful of people moving around bearing torches which they flashed at approaching cars. To this accompaniment, I drove across the bridge to leave my vehicle in the pub's car-park even if it meant going outside my own county boundary; in these conditions, I reckoned it was the safest place to park.

I was surprised that I was able to cross the bridge without hindrance – I had expected to find it blocked or at least obstructed by the vehicles involved in the accident, but the entire road across the bridge was clear and I had no difficulty entering the fogbound carpark. I guessed the problem lay close to where I had seen the car lights and small crowd – perhaps a car had gone through the hedge or run off the road? But even as I eased to a halt and opened the door, I heard a familiar voice.

'By gum, you took your time getting here; it's a good job I wasn't bleeding to death or trapped in a blazing lorry. Oh, it's you, PC Rhea, I wasn't expecting the constabulary and certainly not you, but I might have known you'd take your time getting to summat involving me, but what are you doing out here? You're a long way from Aidensfield. I hope you're not lost in all this fog...'

'And I might have known you'd be mixed up in such sort of skulduggery on a dark and foggy night, Claude.' The familiar shape of Greengrass hitched his old coat tightly around himself. 'Anyway, I had no idea you were involved so where are the vehicles?'

'What vehicles?'

I was out of my GP car by this time, and placing my cap on my head, took a powerful torch from the boot and was preparing to assess the situation, wherever it was. 'I was told there was a non-injury accident on Thorburn Bridge, so here I am, ready to deal with it and take particulars.'

'Who told you that?' He looked genuinely surprised at my comment.

'I got a call from our Control Room,' I told him. 'Are you saying there is no accident?'

'It all depends what you mean by accident.' He grinned wickedly. 'It'd be some bright spark in the pub, ringing up in a panic due to all that banging and clattering... I never called the police, it wasn't that sort of accident, but now you're here, you can flash that blue light of yours when the crane arrives, to stop oncoming cars and keep folks back ... it won't be easy, in all this fog and darkness...'

'Claude, I have no idea what you're talking about.'

'I thought you said your Control Room had told you?' he said in all honesty.

'I was told there was a non-injury accident at this location, that's all; I was not given any details. So how about you enlightening me before it gets complicated. Are you saying there hasn't been an accident?'

'Well, like I said, it all depends on what you mean by accident. All I want to do is get my henhouse out of that river before it gets washed away and broken up with all that fresh water...'

'Henhouse?' I said.

'It fell off the back of my lorry.' He now began to look sheepish. Already, I was considering whether or not he'd had an insecure load, which was a road traffic offence. And he knew what I was thinking.

'Fell off?' I sought confirmation of this.

'Well, jumped off more like. It was empty, I might add, no hens on board, or eggs in nest boxes. No livestock to get hurt. I've rung Bernie Scripps at his garage and told him to get here quick with that crane on his breakdown truck and we can hoick it out of the river while it's still in one piece. I had a look before you got here ... if you shine your torch over the parapet you can see it. It fell in the water where it's deep, so it's not broken up, and a big rock's stopping it being washed downstream. But if we get a few

25

more inches of fast and fresh water, it could shift it and once it starts to move, it'll soon break up...'

'Wouldn't it be sensible to leave it until daylight tomorrow?' I suggested.

'Not likely, not with all that fresh water coming off the moors; there might be a flood before morning and if the level rises, it'll wash my henhouse away and break it up. Anyroad, Bernie's on his way now; those folks at the other side of the bridge are waiting for him, to show him where it is and give a hand while I make sure it's not washed away.'

I now felt a little more clearer about the circumstances, but had not yet established whether or not another vehicle had been involved.

'So, Claude, how did all this happen?' I put to him.

'I'd been over to Driffield to buy the henhouse at a farm sale, and put it on the back of my flat-bed wagon. It was roped on, but with all this fog and muck I hit this bridge just a bit too fast. As you know, it's a long straight run, and a fast one, down from the Wolds, and this bridge has a bit of a hump in the middle, but with this riverside fog I didn't realize I'd got to the bridge. I was moving at a fair speed...'

'I trust your brakes were working!' I said.

'I can do without you getting all official,' he said. 'Anyhow, that bridge is more like a humpback than a level bridge and when I got to the middle, my front wheels took off and when they landed, with the rear wheels following suit, it shook the henhouse off the back. It's very heavy and bulky, and the rope snapped; then with all that movement, it toppled over the parapet, straight into the water...'

'But there was no other vehicle involved?' I asked.

'No, luckily there was nowt on the bridge at the time and the water's deep enough to stop the henhouse getting smashed to smithereens. Anyroad, I went into the pub to ring Bernie and the folks in there had heard the clatter and already rung for the police. I said all I wanted was a breakdown but some nosy sod had already rung your lot.'

'Good,' I smiled, thinking of our accident statistics. 'For my purposes, it's not a reportable road accident, so I don't want to get involved. Henhouse recovery is not really a matter for the police, and besides you're not on my patch. Right where we are now, we're over the border, in the East Riding.'

'It's a matter of debate, is it, whether my henhouse fell into the East Riding or the North Riding?' began Claude.

'It is, and as I'm from the North Riding, Claude, and there is no East Riding constable here, I suggest it has fallen into the East Riding.'

'Has it? I can't see it matters to me. All that matters so far as I'm concerned is that Bernie should be here soon,' he said. 'Wherever you're from, it might be a good idea if you stayed and used that blue light of yours while we're lifting it out of the beck, you know, to prevent accidents in all this fog.'

It was a good idea, if only to try and prevent an accident on the bridge during the recovery operation. To cut short a long story, Bernie, with a helping hand from the volunteers who had so patiently waited, did succeed in lifting the henhouse out of the river with his crane and it was replaced securely on Claude's old flat-bed truck. We had an audience from the pub too, and a queue of patiently waiting drivers.

It was all over in a surprisingly short time. Afterwards, everyone adjourned to the Salmon for a celebratory drink – Claude borrowed the money from Bernie, saying he'd spent all his cash buying the henhouse, but I did not join them. I could not drink alcohol in uniform – and most certainly not in a pub off my own patch. The fact that the pub might stay open after hours was no concern of mine – county boundaries can be useful and this pub was not in our police area. In any case, I was now working over-time and so I provided a situation report to Control, confirming that it was not a road traffic accident within the meaning of the law. I knew the officer-in-charge would be relieved – our impressive record would not be jeopardized. It was almost midnight by the time I booked off duty and I was later to learn there were no recorded traffic accidents during those final minutes of 30 September.

Next morning, though, Sergeant Craddock telephoned me in my office.

'Ah, PC Rhea.' He sounded cheerful. 'I've had the superintendent on the line, he says you did a good job last night, keeping accidents at bay. He has told me about the incident on Thorburn Bridge – outside my section as it happens – and he has read your preliminary account. He has asked me to tell you that he's expecting an offence report to be submitted against Claude Jeremiah Greengrass. He wants him prosecuted for having an insecure load on his motor vehicle and you might even consider the vehicle and its load were in a dangerous condition.'

'Ah, well, the incident happened on the East Riding side of the bridge, Sergeant, out of our jurisdiction. No East Riding officers attended and there is no evidence left at the scene now.'

'So it is not our problem?'

'No, Sergeant.'

'Good, I will inform the superintendent. It's nice to have a clean sheet, is it not? No outstanding reports of any kind?'

'Most certainly, Sergeant,' I agreed.

Chapter 2

One of the people I noticed regularly around Aidensfield was Jenny Lockwood, a heavily built, blonde-haired woman in her late thirties. Always with a happy expression on her round pink face, she lived on the council estate, at No. 4, Elsinby View. She boasted a family of five small children, a husband who was usually out of work, a couple of spaniels and a cat called Minnie. Her husband, Arthur, a large untidy but very affable man known locally as Arty, spent much of his time in bed or in the pub but even during those periods when he was not working (and there were many), he managed to raise sufficient funds to join his mates in the bar, buy a round or two, and gamble on the outcome of dominoes, darts and horse races. I'm sure he lost more than he won.

Of the two, Jenny was certainly the worker and far more dependable; most of us thought Arty scrounged money from his wife to spend in the pub. Even with her family of youngsters, she managed to find lots of part-time jobs, especially when Arty was either too idle or too unfortunate to be in work. As most of the jobs paid cash, Jenny probably avoided unsavoury things like income tax and National Insurance contributions and, as most of the money was apparently spent on the children and the home, no one seemed to criticize her dependency on a personal and somewhat miniature black economy.

It was known that her home was well kept, clean and nicely furnished, her children were always beautifully dressed and polite, and she managed to drive a very splendid Singer Vogue estate car, second-hand, but in superb condition.

A beautiful navy-blue colour, it was always well maintained and was spacious enough to accommodate Jenny and her lively youngsters – and Arty too, whenever he consented to join his family on an outing. There was plenty of room in the back for her dogs or whatever else required transportation. In her rather up-market lifestyle, Jenny paid all her bills, too. The shop, post office, pub and butcher never had to press for payment because she paid cash at the time of her purchases and never ran up accounts; furthermore, she always made sure that matters like the electricity bill, telephone account and rent were never overdue. Those of us who knew Jenny felt that, in spite of her many-faceted career, she must have some kind of additional personal income – from her parents perhaps, or even a legacy of some kind which she never made public. I felt that her galaxy of part-time jobs, however well paid, would not enable her to live quite so well as she did, even if her husband had been in full-time employment. That she was a busy woman was not in question; she did work hard; she was always hurrying from one job to another and had little or no time to join village activities – she was far too busy to bother with things like joining the WI, church flower-arranging or the debating society, but she was always cheerful and seemed very content with life.

There was little doubt that most of us regarded Jenny with some kind of awe – those of us, like me and my family, could not afford the high-quality clothes she bought for her youngsters; we could not afford to run such a smart vehicle. We all felt she had found a magic formula which allowed her to generate sufficient money to meet all her needs whilst not being flashy or extravagant.

She didn't buy cheap stuff either – she always bought goods of real quality and did not throw away her money on frivolous and useless things. She never played bingo, for example, but did take her holidays in places like Skegness or Blackpool. When spending in the local shops, she always had an eye for a bargain and was willing to barter. She was particularly vociferous if she felt something was overpriced.

A lot of other young mothers – and dads – regarded Jenny as some kind of icon, someone who set a good example to the rest of the village, a hard-working woman who could manage money very capably in addition to coping with a ne'er-do-well husband.

Oddly enough, one reason for the successful management of her affairs was due to her husband being at home for much of the time. It meant he could care for the children, do the housework, keep the garden tidy and even go shopping for groceries – all of which he did reasonably well – and in turn, that left Jenny free to pursue her multi-layered career of umpteen part-time occupations. I don't know how she juggled those either – among her jobs, she was an office cleaner at a bank in Ashfordly (a 6 a.m.-7.30 a.m. morning task), a waitress, a barmaid, an assistant to a local vet, a chambermaid, a dog walker, house-sitter, baby-sitter, Avon lady, cake-maker, dinner lady at a school, clerk at council and general elections, market-stall worker – and more besides. One or two jobs were in Aidensfield a few were in Ashfordly but most of them were well away from the locality, in places like Middlesbrough, York, Scarborough, Thirsk, Malton and Stokesley.

In her smart car, I would sometimes see her dashing out of the village to some appointment or other, or see her dashing back afterwards, eager to have a wash and change of clothing before rushing off to some other job or, as she termed it, professional engagement. And, I must admit, she always seemed cheerful and full of energy.

I suppose, in a way, she was a self-employed person, hiring out her skills to those who were prepared to pay and, like so many self-employed people, she appeared to enjoy her life in spite of being so busy. For Jenny, management of her time and income was important and most of the villagers agreed she seemed to be very successful at both. On rare occasions when she was in between jobs, I would come across her in Aidensfield, usually leaving the post office or shop, or sometimes walking her dogs along the street, and, like all the village people, she was happy to stop for a chat. We'd pass the time of day quite affably, with me asking where she was working now, how her family was faring and what her husband was doing.

'Oh, I've got a little job on Teesside now, Mr Rhea,' she might say. 'Two afternoons a week in a dress shop. It's a long way but the money's good.' Or she would say, 'I'm dashing off to Ashfordly, I'm looking after an old lady while her daughter's gone out to get her hair done ... three hours...' Or, 'I have to go into York, they're short of a waitress in that new coffee shop in Mickle-gate and I said could do an occasional afternoon for them...' Or, 'They want someone to feed the hens and dogs at High Rigg Farm on the moors above Stokesley while the owners are in London...' Or 'I've got a job in that new off-licence in Malton, two evenings a week...'

Occasionally, if she had the time, she would spend a little longer chatting to me and on one occasion, I commented, 'With all those jobs in places like York and Teesside, Jenny, wouldn't it pay you to live nearer one of the bigger conurbations? As things are, the travelling must be expensive and time-consuming, and if you were closer, you'd probably get some kind of full-time employment.'

'Oh, I couldn't do that, Mr Rhea,' she cried. 'Live in a town? Not me! Give me the countryside any day. I don't mind working in a town, for a short time, but once I get back over Brantgate Bridge and on to those moors, I know I'm nearly home and I can relax. That's my boundary, Brantgate Bridge – when I see that, I know the grime of industry and the noise and greyness of the town is behind me and that I'll be home before too long ... it's worth the extra few bob I spend on petrol.'

I knew Brantgate Bridge very well. It did not mark the boundary of my beat, but it was the boundary of the subdivision in which Aidensfield and Ashfordly were located. It was not a county boundary either, but it did herald a distinction of sorts because the flatness of the landscape to the north of the moors ended close to the bridge. It might even be said that Brantdale began at that bridge, and from there it cut deep into the moors to produce a picturesque and remote dale. Upon leaving the bridge, however, the road skirted the side of the hill, avoiding both the lowest and highest ground as it carried traffic from the industrial area of Teesside into the heather-clad moorland, and thence to Ashfordly, Aidensfield and beyond. Because Brantgate Bridge was our sub-divisional boundary, it featured quite regularly in our daily routine.

It was a convenient rendezvous point, for example, when the inspector would call us and say, 'I'll meet you at Brantgate Bridge' which was his way of establishing a nice official outing for himself while ensuring that we constables patrolled the far extremities of our sub-division. And so, if I received such a call, I would motor out to the bridge, park my vehicle and await the rendezvous. If I had time to while away, I'd stand upon the centremost point, either gazing into the clear waters beneath to watch the fish, eels and waterlife, or else to stare, often in wonder, at the splendour of the lofty, craggy and stunningly beautiful purple moors which surrounded me. Skylarks could be heard singing aloft, and sometimes the cry of a curlew or the chatter of a grouse would complement the character of the windswept dale.

There was a history to the bridge, of course. I discovered there had been a ford here in medieval times, and so far as I could ascertain, the bridge had first appeared towards the end of the seventeenth century, albeit not in its current form. It had then been a narrow packhorse bridge, scarcely wide enough to accommodate a laden cart, and, over the years, it had been demolished, widened, swept away by floods, replaced, rebuilt and modernized to the extent that it was now a wide, handsome and fairly modern bridge with stone parapets and footpaths beside the carriageway. It has had its share of drama too – there had been a drowning here in the early nineteenth century, when a young woman had tried to wade the flooded river because the bridge had been swept away. She died in the raging river and it is said that on Hallowe'en, the anniversary of her death, the ghost of Rebecca Harland haunts the bridge even now.

A runaway horse once leapt over the parapet too, and was killed, while, during the Second World War, a military despatch rider came to grief here, rushing to deliver some urgent message to a nearby army camp. He failed to take the corner which precedes the bridge on the Ashfordly side. But in all the time I was at Aidensfield, there were no untoward incidents on or near Brantgate Bridge, not even a road traffic accident or an instance of flooding. For me, it marked a boundary and nothing more. And then I received a telephone call from Detective Sergeant Howard Bedford of Eltering CID.

'Nick.' His call came on a Wednesday evening and I took it in the office which was attached to my police house. 'Howard Bedford here. I need a uniform constable to take part in an exercise tomorrow. Can you make yourself available? It'll be during the afternoon, three o'clock or thereabouts. For no longer than a couple of hours, if things go as planned.'

I checked my desk diary and, as I had no previous commitments, I said, 'Yes, Sergeant, I can come along, I've no commitments.'

'Good. Keep the afternoon clean I'll contact you tomorrow morning with your instructions. Till then, say nothing to anyone, although I shall alert your Sergeant Craddock that I shall require you, and he will be told that if anything else crops up, like a traffic accident, he'll have to find someone else to deal with it.'

'Very good, Sergeant,' I responded very formally, wondering what on earth was going to happen.

'Till tomorrow then,' he said. 'I'll be in touch in the morning.'

And without any further explanation, he replaced the telephone. I was off duty that evening and must admit I spent a good deal of time trying to guess the nature of my forthcoming task but, understandably, failed to produce any kind of positive answer. However, two factors were evident first, Bedford had described the work as an exercise – and I reckoned that must be some kind of raid on a thief's premises or storage depot, and second, he wanted me in uniform. Uniformed constables were necessary at incidents during which a breach of the peace might occur – theirs was a peace-keeping presence, usually in the background. One example was attending the execution of some warrants which entailed bailiffs breaking into houses – the police usually got blamed for such an operation even if it was executed by another agency. I wondered if a warrant was to be executed tomorrow, perhaps a search of some kind with me on guard to emphasize the legality of the proceedings and to prevent any breach of the peace? Another likely reason for the presence of a uniformed constable was to stop a motor vehicle on a road – like ordinary civilians, plain-clothes detectives did not have the power to stop vehicles on public roads and I wondered if that was to be my mission? But I could only wait and see; whatever my duties, tomorrow promised an interesting break from routine.

At nine next morning, my phone rang and it was Sergeant Craddock. 'Ah, PC Rhea,' he said. 'I do believe Detective Sergeant Bedford has already been in touch with you?'

'Yes, Sergeant,' I acknowledged. 'He wants me to take part in an exercise this afternoon.'

'Good, well, so long as you are aware of that. I was just checking that you knew about it, he did talk it over with me and I shall not put obstacles in your way.'

'Thanks, Sergeant.'

'So, er, what is this exercise, PC Rhea? Any idea? It seems all very hush-hush.'

'I don't know,' I told him. 'I'm awaiting instruction. He's not told me anything about it. I don't even know where I have to go.'

'Ah, well, it must be something very important and rather delicate, eh? Some kind of secret or sensitive CID operation. Well, I won't keep you. Do your best to uphold the honour of Ashfordly section, whatever the exercise happens to be.'

'I will, Sergeant,' and I smiled as I concluded that call; it was evident I was not the only person unaware of what was about to happen. Ten minutes later, the phone rang again and this time it was Howard Bedford.

'All set, Nick?' he put to me.

'Ready when you are, Sergeant,' I said.

'You've got the Mini-van today?' he asked.

'Yes, I'm on a nine-to-five duty with it.'

'Good, well, I want you to go to Brantgate Bridge. Be there no later than 2.45 this afternoon, in uniform as I mentioned earlier.'

'Right,' I agreed. 'No problem, Sergeant.'

'Good, I will rendezvous with you at the bridge; Cliff Cooper will be there too.'

'I know Cliff,' I said, Cliff being a detective constable from Eltering.

'Fine. Well, it's a simple job, Nick, all we want you to do is to stop some cars coming down Brantdale – we'll identify them – we want to carry out a search or two. I'll give

43

you full instructions when we get there.'

'Right, Sergeant.'

'And keep this under your hat!' he said. 'Not a word to anyone. See you there.'

And once again, he rang off with no further explanation.

Whatever the operation, it seemed that my part was a fairly small one – I was there to do a spot of traffic duty – but I had no idea what else was involved. That morning, therefore, I performed a patrol around Aidensfield, Elsinby, Crampton and Lower Keld with a few routine visits to farms and estate offices, went home for lunch, and then departed for Brantdale and its bridge. I arrived two or three minutes ahead of the appointed time, parked on a small gravelled area close to the bridge, emerged from the van and awaited my contacts. As I had done many times before, I found myself gazing into the clear water of Brantdale Beck, watching the ripples as it ran over a bed of rounded stones and gravel, smoothing underwater weeds and eddying in places where a larger rock provided a barrier to its flow. Behind me, across the moors, a skylark was singing somewhere high in the heavens; the sky was almost cloudless and the sun was bathing the landscape with a warm blanket of air, but I could not see that aerial songster, known locally as the laverock. He was high enough to be well beyond my vision but his free and wild music was wonderfully evocative of the wide open spaces around me.

And then two unmarked cars appeared from the opposite direction, one driven by Bedford and the other by Cooper. They eased into the parking area where I had left my van, and the two detectives climbed out.

'Hi, Nick,' greeted Bedford whom I had known for several years. He was in his late thirties, a stout, no-nonsense detective who dressed like a farmer. Cooper, five years his junior and looking rather like a bank clerk, also exchanged pleasantries with me, then Bedford came to the purpose of our visit.

'It's a simple operation from your point of view,' he told me. 'All we want is a couple of cars to be stopped. It's likely they'll be driving in convoy. Once they're stationary, Cliff and I will search them. We need you to bring them to a halt and guide them off the road; we did a recce earlier and there's a convenient field just behind you; we'll open the gate. There are no cattle so you can guide the cars into it ... that'll get the cars off the road which makes our job easier, and

45

it'll also stop the drivers doing a runner! We'll follow them into the field, then you can close the gate and keep them in!'

'It would make sense for me to position the van halfway across the carriageway, then? Near that gate, then I can direct them into the field and let the other traffic continue.'

'Right. Now, the two cars in question. Cliff and I will park in that picnic area at the top of Brantgate Bank. We'll have a good view of the road as it climbs from Teesside and we'll see the two cars approaching. We'll be told when they leave Middlesbrough and they'll reach us four or five minutes before they get to you.'

I knew the hilltop in question, it provided spectacular views of the dale with its road winding its way along the hillside. 'I know the place,' I assured them.

'Good. Now, as they reach us, I shall call you on the radio – I'll need your call-sign – and that's the cue for you to position your van in the road and to do your traffic cop act. As the two cars pass us, though, we will follow them; as they approach you, therefore, we'll be directly behind. We'll sit on their tails and, as there are no crossroads, junctions or lanes leading off, unless they turn around, they must come to you. And in the very unlikely event of them turning around, we'll follow them in unmarked cars – or follow one of them as they case may be.'

'You'll give me a description of them?' I asked.

'I can do that now,' said Bedford. 'One of them is a navy blue Singer Vogue estate car,' and he provided the registration number. 'It will be driven by a heavily built woman, name of Jenny Lockwood. The other is a Hillman Minx estate car in a tan shade, and it will be driven by another woman called Joanna Robson...'

I was hardly listening now; the shock of hearing Jenny's name and a description of her car had momentarily made me lose my concentration, and I interrupted Bedford.

'Sorry, Sarge,' I heard myself say. 'Did you say Jenny Lockwood?'

'She lives on your patch, I believe?' He smiled ruefully.

'Yes, that's why I did a double-take ... so what's she up to?'

'Shoplifting on a major scale, Nick, with the Robson woman. They drive into a town, separately, and select a chain store, usually with childrens' clothes ... they nick as much as they can carry, split as they make their getaway to baffle a solitary store detective, then get taxis back to where they have parked their cars, in different locations a long way from the stores. They rent lock-up garages by the week so they can hide their cars inside them. They change into some different outer clothes, emerge and if the coast is clear, they go home and sell their loot. They've ready markets for the clothes – and other items they manage to nick – but Middlesbrough Police have been tailing them for weeks now, establishing their routine and so on. We need to catch them red-handed, in possession of stolen property because usually they manage to either dodge the police or store detectives, or ditch the property before they're caught ... so this time, we're letting them drive nearly home. This is one of their days, you see, for 'working' in Middlesbrough, doing little jobs in clothes shops! We know that. We know they got there this morning. We know where they left their cars. It's just a case of waiting for Middlesbrough to tell us they're on the way home and this time, we'll be waiting.'

'I can't believe Jenny would do that ... she seems such a decent, hard-working mother...'

'She's hard-working all right, Nick. She

never stops ... York, Middlesbrough, Scarborough, you name it, she's been there to nick stuff from department stores like Marks and Spencer, Debenhams, Binns ... and even little shops like specialist childrens' clothes dealers, shoe shops and so on. She's an expert, Nick, believe me. We've been tailing her as well other forces. She's clever, very clever. She does hold down one or two proper part-time jobs, as a cover for driving away from home, and she never operates near home, and she always pays her bills, to stop anyone taking an interest in her finances ... she's a professional, Nick. But today, we're going to be just as professional as she is!'

They remained with me for another twenty minutes or so, going over the precise details several times to ensure we all knew what to do, then Bedford said, 'Right, well, Nick, time we were moving. They're due to leave Middlesbrough about now, this is their regular routine. That gives us half an hour or so. Come on, Cliff, let's get parked up at the Bank Top and pretend to be tourists.'

Still reeling from their revelations, I went and sat in the van to make sure I heard any radio messages. I heard the detectives record their arrival at Brantdale Bank Top and then Bedford called me, just as a test call. I responded to say I was receiving their signal loud and clear and then settled down for an indeterminate wait, alone with my thoughts. The dale was very quiet with very little traffic and, as I brooded over Jenny's behaviour, including the quality of her family's clothes and her easy lifestyle, I realized the signals had all been there. Her demeanour had attracted comment. All of us, including me, had wondered how she could afford to live in the way she did, with only part-time jobs to sustain her – and now I knew the reason. I wondered how her friends in the village would react to the news there'd be an arrest, a search of her home and any other premises she used, and the inevitable court appearance. The village was in for an unwelcome shock.

Then my radio burbled into life. I responded. As anticipated, the Singer and the Hillman were now passing over Brantdale Bank Top; Bedford confirmed their descriptions and registration numbers and I responded by saying I would establish my road block. At that stage, the two unmarked CID cars took up their positions to the rear of the suspects and began shadowing them down the dale. I wondered if Jenny and her friend would realize the police were tailing them ... hopefully, they'd think the cars belonged to tourists. This development meant I had only a few minutes to establish my check point. It was the work of a moment to position the Mini-van at an angle across the road with its blue light flashing, and I selected a part of the road upon which I could stand to guide other cars through, but direct the two suspects into the convenient field.

It seemed only seconds before I spotted the oncoming vehicles. They crested a rise about half a mile away and I stepped into the road ahead of them. A solitary white van was the first to reach me and I guided it through with a wave of my hand, the expression on the driver's face showing his bewilderment at the sight of a constable standing in the middle of an isolated road with the apparent purpose of directing a single vehicle around his own parked van. I had no idea what conclusion he drew from those moments, but it was now the turn of the Singer Vogue. With the farm gate standing wide open, I directed Jenny into the field. She obeyed even if the expression on her face revealed her utter surprise – and some apprehension – at this development.

Then her friend followed. The two CID cars did likewise and, as Jenny stepped from her car to question my action, Howard Bedford was there to greet her.

I closed the gate and stood by it, leaving the van momentarily in the road with its blue light flashing, but the handful of vehicles using the road negotiated it without a problem. I've no doubt they associated its presence with the four cars oddly parked in the roadside field. As the two women stood helplessly by, Bedford and Cooper began to search their estate cars and found that each rear portion was boarded over with a false floor, under which were dozens of children's dresses and other clothes.

The two women were arrested; they were placed in one of the CID cars whose doors could not be unlocked from the inside, and Cliff Robson drove them to Eltering Police Station, there to be charged and kept in the cells until the full extent of their thieving was known. As they emerged from the field, Jenny, on the nearside of the rear seat, stared directly into my eyes and I wondered if she thought I had engineered her arrest. Bedford remained with the two cars, each full of incriminating evidence, and he said, 'You can go now, Nick. I've called Eltering;

they're sending a couple of drivers out to help me remove these estate cars. We've got enough evidence to have those women prosecuted, but it'll only be specimen charges. They've been at it for years ... and this won't stop them. Shoplifting is like a disease – once it's in the blood, you can't get rid of it.'

And so I left the scene, switching off my blue flashing light as I drove back down the dale from Brantgate Bridge. The skylark was still singing as I drove away, but as Jenny herself had told me, once I was on this side of Brantgate Bridge, I felt I was home. For her, of course, this day's crossing of that bridge did herald her return home – albeit with a visit to a police cell *en route.*

It was a sad homecoming for her, and a severe shock, but she deserved it. Three months later, she received a suspended sentence of three years' imprisonment upon which she and her family moved closer to York. Her criminal record and reputation accompanied her, with York police being made aware of her potentially dishonest activities. I was delighted she was no longer living in Aidensfield, but as a matter of record, she was caught again, just one year later, stealing from Woolworths in York.

I don't think Jenny Lockwood was able to prevent herself stealing from shops and although much of the stuff she acquired served a useful purpose, either because it was resold to unwitting customers, or used by her own family, she stole a considerable amount of useless objects which she kept at home. The CID found those when they searched her house – there were things like a whole range of cheap and tacky souvenirs from seaside gift shops, umpteen boxes of Elastoplast and tubes of toothpaste, shoe-laces, glass ornaments and china oddments, plastic teaspoons by the hundred, ten cards of watchstraps, second-hand knitting needles by the score, three dozen cork-screws, tins of soup and baked beans which looked as if they'd been found in the river, and more besides. The hidden recesses of her home were like a series of Aladdin's caves and it was clear she was a klepto-maniac as well as a shoplifter.

As I was to discover, however, she was not the only kleptomaniac on my patch.

Another was an elderly gentleman called Bert Hobbleston who lived alone in the miniscule Bridge End Cottage at Elsinby. He had never married and had spent his working life as a farm labourer and general contractor in and around the district. He was in his late seventies when we became acquainted, and soon I discovered he was considered an expert on the subject of heavy horses, being a regular judge of Shire and Clydesdale classes at local agricultural shows. A chatty character of medium height with a round, happy face, he sported a mop of long and somewhat dirty grey hair upon which he perched a black beret, and he had a habit of always wearing the same greasy dark-grey suit, summer and winter alike. But he had one odd habit – he never wore socks.

In the summer months, he took to wearing sandals, albeit without casting aside his old grey suit, but in the cooler seasons he wore large black boots – always without socks. Although I talked to him quite frequently and found him affable and interesting, particularly when the conversation turned to his beloved heavy horses, he never revealed the reason for this habit. It would have been quite acceptable in a Mediterranean resort, but I thought it was somewhat peculiar for an elderly man living on the edge of the North York Moors. The villagers never mentioned it – most of them had grown up with the notion that Bert never wore socks and they accepted it as quite normal. In time, of course, I grew to accept this quirk as normal and regarded it as part of Bert's character; I realized I had fully accepted it as I reached the stage where the situation ceased to intrigue me and when I found myself not wanting to ask any of the locals if there was an explanation for Bert's eccentricity.

Another of his characteristics was to spend rather too long in the pub and to drink rather too many pints of best bitter. Most nights, Bert could be seen staggering home along the side of the road which led from the Hopbind Inn to his tiny cottage, a matter of about 400 yards. There was no footpath and a shallow stream ran along one side of the road – many of us wondered whether Bert ever missed his footing and fell into the water during those nightly excursions, but it seems he did not. If he had fallen in, I doubt it would have been a disaster – the water was only three or four inches deep and unless he tumbled in face down and unconscious, he would come to no harm, apart from a thorough soaking. He was never too drunk to stand up or to find his own way home, and he would often sing to himself as he made his way to Bridge End Cottage. He did not sing so loudly that it became a nuisance; rather, it was a type of serenade sung in a low voice as he made his way to bed. For most people, the sound of Bert's singing during his post-drinking trek formed part of the atmosphere of an evening in Elsinby and, of course, it indicated he was fit and well, and safely plodding homewards.

As the village constable, I was aware of Bert's character traits and whenever I was patrolling in the late evening, I would endeavour to make a discreet check that no harm had come to him. I'd toot my horn if I passed him, or I'd check that the lights had come on in his house after closing time, or that he was not lying injured on the roadside or in the beck – those were the kind of checks that any rural constable would make during his rounds in this kind of situation.

But one night, Bert had an accident.

I was not in Elsinby at the time because I was performing a late duty outside the village hall in Crampton where a Young Farmers' Dance was under way. My police van was prominently parked outside the hall, itself a deterrent to bad and loutish behaviour, and its radio was switched on I heard my call sign and responded to discover that Bert Hobbleston had been found lying in the beck at Elsinby with injuries to his head, and he had been taken into a nearby house, 12 Beckside. An ambulance had been called, and the local GP, Dr Archie McGee, had been summoned to the scene. Control told me there was a suggestion of a hit-and-run traffic accident with Bert as the casualty, so I abandoned my supervision of the dance hall and assured Control I would get there as soon as I could, giving my estimated time of arrival as within six or seven minutes.

When I arrived, I found a knot of worried looking people standing outside 12 Beckside, but no sign of the ambulance. As I rushed to the house, I made a quick examination of the road in the lights of my van, trying to see if there was any sign of glass or debris from a vehicle, or even tyre skid-marks on the road surface, but I found nothing. Tomorrow, I would make a more rigorous search in daylight.

'He's in there,' someone called to me. 'With the doctor.'

I rushed into the house to find Bert lying on the kitchen floor in clothes dripping with water and covered with soft brown mud. Dr

McGee was examining him. I was not surprised to find him like this – to have placed him on a settee in the lounge, or on a bed upstairs, would have caused immense cleaning-up problems for the lady of the house!

Besides, the doctor would cope better with him on the floor and there had been some effort to make him comfortable – someone had produced a groundsheet for a medium-sized tent, and that was beneath Bert's still form. It was covering the kitchen rug upon which he lay and he was as comfortable as possible in the circumstances. He was in a grossly filthy state and was unconscious, but the doctor was saying, 'He's had a nasty bump, but whether he got that by falling into the beck and hitting his head on a rock, or whether he was knocked over by a passing car or lorry, well, I just don't know.'

Dr McGee loosened some of Bert's clothing and made a physical examination of other parts of his body, but found nothing – except a rather pungent smell which was made worse by the effects of the river water.

Then someone called, 'The ambulance is here, Doctor.'

'Right, get them to fetch a stretcher in; I

think he should go to hospital for a check-up. I think it's concussion and a few abrasions, nothing too serious, but I'd like him to be given the all-clear by experts.'

A pair of ambulancemen, with a stretcher at the ready, were shown into the kitchen and Bert was gently placed upon it and covered with an official blanket as the doctor said, 'Take him to Casualty, please. It's either a hit-and-run accident, or a nasty fall in which he suffered those wounds to the head, and possible concussion. I can't find any other evident injuries, his breathing is OK and his heart is working well. This is not a panic situation.'

'He hasn't any socks on,' one of the ambulancemen pointed out.

'No, he never wears them,' smiled a by-stander.

'Ah, well, it takes all sorts. Has he any next-of-kin?' the ambulancemen then asked of anyone who might provide an answer. I realized everyone was looking at me.

'Not to my knowledge,' I shook my head. 'He lives alone. He's not married, but I really don't know much about his personal life.'

A woman piped up. 'There's nobody,' she confirmed. 'I've never heard him mention

60

family at all.'

'I'll search the house,' I said. 'He might have a list of addresses somewhere.'

'You'll need the key,' one of the ambulancemen said. 'You'd better have it before we leave!' and he began to hunt through Bert's pockets.

'No need,' said the woman who had spoken earlier. 'He never locks the place...'

'There's nothing in his pockets anyway, just some cash and a dirty old handkerchief,' responded the man.

'I'll go now,' I told them. 'I'll secure the house when I leave; we don't want anyone going in during Bert's absence.'

'I can't say I'd want to go into that place!' I heard a woman whisper. 'I don't know the last time he cleaned up, I once got as far as his kitchen and the smell ... urrrgh...'

And so, with a minimum of fuss, Bert was placed in the ambulance and it sped its smooth way towards York County Hospital, but without its blue light flashing. This was not that kind of emergency; Bert was not in a critical condition. I would ring tomorrow for an update on his progress but in the meantime, I wanted a word with Dr McGee and any possible witnesses. A few villagers, neighbours and pub regulars, were still hanging around.

I asked of anyone who might answer, 'Did anyone see what happened? Did a vehicle come past when Bert was on the road? Anyone hear brakes being slammed on or a horn blowing? Shouting? Banging noises? Anything unusual?'

It took a few minutes for me to establish that no one had seen any kind of incident which would support the theory that Bert had been hit by a passing vehicle. When I pressed Dr McGee for his opinion, he tended towards a view that Bert had tripped and fallen into the beck, landing headfirst and crashing his skull against a large rock – and there were plenty in the bed of the beck and others were concealed in the under-growth along its banks. The lack of other marks on his body, and in the absence of damage to his suit or vehicle marks on his clothing, and with no particles of glass or paint adhering to any part of him or his clothes, made it seem Bert was not the victim of a hit-and-run driver. Taking every-thing into account, I veered towards the belief that he had tumbled into the beck whilst unsteady through his habitual drink-ing, but I would check at the pub tomorrow, to try and ascertain his actual state upon leaving the premises.

I thanked everyone for their part in tonight's response and Dr McGee said he would send his written report to me within a few days so I could complete my file of the incident. He confirmed he would support the notion that Bert had tripped and fallen, and appeared to be suffering from concussion.

As they all wended their way home, I walked along the beckside to Bert's little cottage, now in darkness. I would make a quick search for any contact addresses and then secure the house as best I could. I entered through the kitchen door (Yorkshire folk rarely use the front door) and shone my torch to find a light switch but already I was aware of a foul smell wafting from one of the other rooms. I found the switch and pressed it. The kitchen was a small, untidy place with a tiny table and chair against one wall, a sink under the window and a blue painted store cupboard near another wall. There were pots and pans in the sink, all unwashed but I was not here to worry about his domestic behaviour – I wanted to know if he had relatives who should be told about his dilemma and the most obvious place to store an address book was that cabinet. But all it contained was a few items of chipped crockery, some old pieces of cutlery and a stale loaf. It boasted a couple of drawers, but they contained bits of official paper – his rate demand for example, and electricity accounts, all paid. I think Bert ate at the pub once in a while, which explained his lack of food in store. As I scoured the cabinet, I realized there was no list of addresses.

The lounge was next, or sitting-room as most country folk termed it. But as I opened the door to locate that light switch, I was assailed by the most dreadful smell imaginable. It caught the back of my throat and caused me to cough and splutter as I sought the switch – and, as the bare bulb in the centre of the ceiling illuminated the room, all I saw was a sea of socks. Mens' socks. In all colours. Old ones.

They were piled knee deep on the floor, covering the battered old suite, lying on the window ledge, the hearth, the old sideboard and on the sides of the staircase which rose from a corner of the room. I covered my mouth and nose with one hand as I entered the stinking place wondering how far I would need to search. Unless Bert's address book was hidden under a pile of old socks, there were few other places it might be stored in this room and so I went up the stairs – and every spare surface was piled high with more socks. There was a single bed in one room, with a bedside cabinet, but the whole place was smothered in socks of every size, shape and colour, as was the bathroom, the toilet and the tiny box room at the back of the house ... socks, socks and more socks ... there must have been thousands of them and the stench was unbelievable and eyewatering.

I did make a quick search of the places where a list of addresses was likely to be kept but found absolutely nothing, other than more socks, some looking fairly new and others full of holes and clearly very ancient and smelly. I left as quickly as I could. I found a key hanging on a piece of string behind the front door, switched off the lights and took the key with me. Reeling from my experience, I drove home and wondered if the reek of Bert's house was clinging to my uniform so I went straight into my office, removed my tunic and trousers and left them there. I did not want Bert's aroma in my house. Before booking off for the evening, though, I rang the hospital to enquire after Bert and discovered he had regained consciousness, and that he would be detained for at least thirty-six hours so that further checks could be made.

I told the ward sister that I had the key to his house, and they should regard me as next-of-kin until Bert came home.

'What on earth's happened to you?' Mary gasped as I walked into the lounge, trouserless. The children were in bed and so missed that amazing but far from pretty sight, and so, over a welcome cup of cocoa, I told her my story.

'So where did he get all those socks?' was Mary's question. 'They're not his own, surely?'

'He doesn't wear socks,' I told her. 'But these were dirty and full of holes, or most of them were. But why would anyone hoard old socks?'

'For the wool?' she smiled. 'Or to dress a scarecrow?'

After I had a bath and washed my hair in the hope of eliminating any strong wafts of old socks, we went to bed. Next morning, I was told Bert would remain in hospital for a further day and so, after revisiting the scene to search without result for signs of vehicle debris or tyre-marks, my next calling place was the Hopbind Inn. I hoped I might elicit some kind of explanation for Bert's accident but discovered nothing further – he had been his usual slightly tipsy self upon leaving the bar last night, albeit not troublesome or incapable. Taking everything into account, I felt sure he'd lost his footing near the edge of the beck.

Then I broached the question of the socks.

'His house is full of old socks,' I smiled, as I had a coffee with George Ward, the landlord, in his private office. 'There's a bit of a pong...'

'He collects them,' George told me. 'Don't ask me why, he's never said, but once or twice he was caught searching old bonfires and dustbins, and it turned out he was retrieving socks which had been thrown out.'

'It's not theft if the socks have been abandoned by their owners,' I said. 'And I've had no complaints.'

'He never takes them from washing lines, Nick, they're always cast-offs from wherever he can find them. We've got used to him, he's harmless...'

'I've got the key to his house,' I told George. 'I've told the hospital where it is, and they'll contact me before they release him.'

'We'll see to him, Nick; the village will look after him, even if no one wants to go into his house full of socks. You're not thinking of prosecuting him, are you? For nicking all those socks?'

I shook my head. 'No. I need a formal complaint if I'm to do that, and I don't think anyone will make a formal statement about someone nicking old, holey socks from their dustbins or rubbish dumps, will they?'

'No, they won't. It's just Bert, you see, that's how he is.'

'Right, fine. I'll do nothing. I wonder if he was brought up in one of those households with an old-fashioned gramophone?'

'Why on earth are you asking that?' George puzzled.

'The early gramophones didn't have volume controls, and they used those old horns to produce the sound ... and if children played them too noisily, they were told to put a sock in it. The sock muffled the noise, you see...'

'You're having me on, aren't you?' George looked uncertain about my explanation. 'You mean they pushed a sock down the trumpet thingy to shut off the racket?'

'Yes, but I think it would be a clean sock,'

I smiled.

'So what's all that got to do with Bert?' he asked.

'I've no idea,' I said. 'Well, I must be off. I'll keep in touch.'

Bert came out of hospital the following day, a little shaken but otherwise unharmed, and he returned to his house after I handed over his key. He invited me in for a cup of tea but I declined with as much grace as I could muster. He couldn't remember anything of the incident and we never did find out what really happened that night.

I've not been into his house since and often wonder if all those old socks are still there. And I never found any law, civil or otherwise, which said it was illegal to hoard smelly old socks in one's own home.

Chapter 3

Among the more frequent tasks undertaken by police officers is to take down in writing, official statements from people such as victims, witnesses and suspects of crime. Witnesses to a wide range of incidents from flash-floods to UFOs are also asked to record the event on paper for future historians to discuss and analyse, and so that official statistics may be compiled. In many cases, the police are responsible, either directly or indirectly, for compiling such records. Motorists involved in traffic accidents are likewise asked to make statements and this is done so that there is a written record of the incident should any proceedings, criminal or civil, be contemplated at some future date. Such recordings of traffic accident are likewise fed into the official pool of information so that statistics may be compiled, and road improvement schemes may be authorized.

One of my colleagues, a young constable out on the streets on his very first day of duty, was faced with something of a dilemma when a car full of Chinese, the family of a local restaurant owner, collided with another one full of Spanish students and the only witness was a German tourist. Happily, the necessary interpreters lived nearby (there happened to be a language school just along the road). I also recall some Italians who arrived at a police station to make some kind of malicious complaint but who were shocked to discover that the very senior sergeant who attended them spoke fluent Italian and had understood everything they had plotted and discussed in the reception area. They left with a new respect for English policemen, even if that one did speak Italian with a Yorkshire accent.

During our initial training as very raw recruits, we were advised, where possible, to obtain negative statements from people who may *not* have witnessed an incident in spite of being in the vicinity at the material time. It was surprising, at the scene of any incident, whether major or minor, how many people upon being asked to provide an account of it, would say, 'Never saw a thing, Officer,' but who would later vividly recall every detail, especially when drinking with pals in the pub. A negative statement usually comprised a single sentence which might say, 'I did not see anything' or 'I was facing the other way at the time' – and this kind of on-the-spot instant statement-taking by a police officer did, on many occasions, counteract and render ineffective a subsequent statement by a 'witness' who afterwards 'remembered' things in surprising detail, especially if a friend or member of the family was likely to be prosecuted, and particularly if such a flash of restored memory would provide an alibi or defence.

Perhaps the worst statement with which one might be confronted was known as a dying declaration. In days of yore, when the Christian religion mattered to a high percentage of the population, it was generally assumed that a person who was dying and who *knew* he or she was dying (and then did actually die) – would never tell a lie during those final moments due to the fear of the wrath of the Almighty in eternity thereafter. A statement thus obtained in the dying breath of a witness was held to be pretty powerful stuff and certainly worthy of credence. Dying declarations were acceptable as truthful evidence, even if not taken under oath and even if a dying villain told a pack of vengeful lies in his last moments on this earth.

A dying declaration to the effect that 'I said I'd get that ******* if it was the last thing I did', may be considered a useful admission, while, 'Yes, I killed him as he shot at me', was likewise considered rather effective.

There is no doubt that many criminals are highly skilled at never making statements of any kind. They know that if they say absolutely nothing about anything, the police will have a most difficult task in proving their guilt, involvement in or proximity to a crime. Furthermore, the investigating police are legally bound to tell suspects they need not say anything unless they wish to do so. This is enough to persuade most sensible villains to say absolutely nowt – and then society wonders why undetected crime has risen so rapidly, why criminals make fun of, and usually ignore, the rule of law, and why so many are never prosecuted. In the past, some very cunning villains, upon being arrested or charged, would say, 'It's a fair cop, guv', and if the constable wrote down those words in any official document, no one would believe it. No one actually said that, did they? It was figment of a crime writer's imagination – or was it? But if, in the right circumstances, a villain actually said that, then it would have to be recorded in writing – in spite of the guaranteed wrath of supervisory officers. If such a statement was eventually presented to a court of law, it could be guaranteed that any defence counsel would pounce upon it with a claim that such a thing had never been said.

Taking down a statement in writing demands considerable skills. It should, as far as possible, be taken down in the actual words used by the person making it, although it must be borne in mind that it has to be intelligible.

A simple test is whether it will be understood by everyone who later reads it. If a witness speaks only in the dialect of the North Riding, for example, should I record his statement in that tongue, or should I translate it into standard English? I've often wondered about the reaction if I wrote, in the words of a witness who had seen a farm accident: 'Awd Isaac skelled ower on t'skeuf and brak 'is 'eead again t'swingletree of 'is pleeaf.'

That's why he might say, but in translation, it would read, 'Old Isaac fell on the hillside and banged his head against the splinter bar of his plough.'

And if a man spoke only in monosyllables, or ungrammatically, should I use his actual words or try to render them suitable for legal consumption? You'd hardly get an uneducated person using correct English. For example, if a villain said, 'I never got none of the stolen stuff', did that mean he really did handle the stolen goods, or that he actually got nothing? If he never got none, it must mean he got some – at least, in some minds the double negative becomes a positive (e.g. 'I don't want none of that!') but in the words of many, 'not to get none' means to get nothing. Purists will say that 'not to get none' truthfully means 'to get some', and 'I don't want none' really means 'I do want some'. Such are the pitfalls of recording the exact words of others for legal purposes – at times, their meaning can lead to confusion.

There is the enduring tale of the West Yorkshireman waiting at an automatic railway crossing. In West Yorkshire, the local people use the word 'while' instead of 'until'.

Because the instructions said, 'Wait while lights flash', he waited *until* the lights flashed – and then set off! The wording of the instruction was therefore changed across the nation to read 'Stop when lights show'.

Perhaps one of the worst examples, so far as ambiguity is concerned, was the phrase 'Let him have it, Chris', which was reportedly used during the infamous trial of Christopher Craig and Derek Bentley for the 1953 murder of PC Miles. Craig, then aged 16, had a .45 Colt revolver when he and Bentley were disturbed by police officers on the roof of a warehouse. The rest is criminal history but Bentley is reported to have shouted, 'Let him have it, Chris', whereupon Christopher Craig shot and killed PC Miles. But did Bentley mean 'Surrender the gun' or did he mean, 'Shoot him'? The meaning of those words – and their dreadful outcome – will be forever debated by criminal historians, for they illustrate just how important it is for the police to ensure, to the best of their ability, that the right words (or their correct interpretation) are used in all official statements, written or otherwise.

There is no doubt that good statement-taking is both an art and a skill, but it is one which is often acquired after many years of police experience, coupled with an understanding of linguistic pitfalls and our own inability to make the correct use of our language. Generally, when interviewing a witness, one has to stick to the facts and avoid hearsay, opinions or evidence which might later be inadmissible in court. Occasionally, a witness might unwittingly say something which amounts to the admission of an offence in which case he or she has to be warned, by the police officer, that it is not obligatory to make such a statement.

If such an admission is freely given, then it is admissible in evidence. In spite of such warnings, many have continued to sign statements which amount to confessions of guilt, a wonderful means of clearing up, with the minimum of effort, outstanding crimes or reported offences.

For example, a driver involved in a traffic accident might say, 'I never saw the other car' which might be considered an admission of careless driving. Perhaps a fine example of a purely voluntary statement was the man who walked into a police station and said, 'Officer, I've just killed my wife'. That crime was reported and detected in the same instant. If the man had said,

'I've just murdered my wife', however, it might be a confession to a crime he had not committed – after all, a good defence lawyer might plead that his true crime was the lesser offence of manslaughter. It all depends upon what he had actually done – and under what circumstances.

There are times when one must keep one's mouth shut – motoring organizations, for example, advise us never to say 'Sorry' when involved in a traffic accident because that could be an admission of guilt or evidence of negligence, and it was in this climate that police officers went – and still go – about their work. They endeavour to obtain legitimate and accurate statements so that the due processes of law might function with efficiency. It has to be said that the police service has never wanted innocent persons to be prosecuted, and its officers have always worked hard to bring the guilty to justice. After all, that is our duty. And the writing down of a good witness statement, freely given, is a vital weapon both in the administration of the law and the recording of important data.

It was with such an apparently simple, but in truth a very complex background, and with thoughts of clearing up a dramatic crime in Aidensfield, that I found myself having to take down a written statement from Miss Phyllida Hobday, a grey-haired spinster of the parish who was aged somewhere around the fifty mark and who worked in a solicitor's office in Ashfordly. The law was therefore her profession – although she was not a solicitor, but a secretary – but one hoped that, in her daily work, she had learned something about its procedures.

I knew Phyllida quite well. She was one of the busy people of Aidensfield, belonging to all kinds of organizations such as the Parochial Church Council, the Women's Institute, the Parish Council, various local committees and indeed some from Ashfordly. Usually, she wore a smart grey two-piece, a crisp white blouse and black, medium-heeled shoes, and she looked rather like a headmistress or even an off-duty hospital matron. Several of her spare-time activities brought her into official contact with me, and when we met, we would have long and, I must admit, occasionally puzzling conversations about village matters and other topics in the local or national news. Being a regular contact of mine, I discovered she had a habit of dispensing with the small-talk which served as a prelude to a discussion and it took me a while to realize she expected me to recall conversations we'd had two, three or even six weeks earlier. I think she dealt with other people in a similar manner and, after a while, I grew accustomed to this, and could usually translate her chatter into a meaningful dialogue. Sometimes, though, I found myself baffled by her comments.

To witness a crime committed in Aidensfield was precisely the sort of thing that would happen to Phyllida – she was always out and about. The crime in question occurred one Saturday afternoon when she was enjoying her weekend break from work. Shortly after 4.30 p.m., a motor cyclist eased to a halt outside the butcher's shop in Aidensfield, hoisted his machine on to its rest but left the engine running, then rushed inside. He grabbed the contents of the till, pushed the assistant aside when she tried to halt him, then rushed out, leapt aboard his bike, thrust it from its rest and roared away almost before anyone realized what had happened. It was a swiftly executed snatch; no one was hurt, although the assistant, a young woman called Julie Weldon, was badly shocked, as was the solitary customer

– Phyllida Hobday. Some said it left Phyllida speechless, a rare condition.

The raider got away with £75 in notes, around a month's wage for some of the local people, but he had ignored the loose change. There was a delay of a few minutes while the two women gathered their wits and decided what to do, then Julie dialled 999 and within a few moments, the call was relayed to me as I was patrolling in my Mini-van. I was about three minutes away, gave Control my eta (estimated time of arrival) and said I would look out for the fleeing motor bike as I hurtled (as only a Mini-van can hurtle) across the moors towards the scene of the crime. I did not see the bike nor any suspicious person but within two and a half minutes, I was drawing to a halt outside the shop. I knew that any available description of the motor cycle and its rider would have been circulated by Control – every police station and mobile officer in the vicinity would already be aware of the crime.

Even during those few short moments, however, a small knot of onlookers had gathered even though there was nothing to see and I knew the best way to disperse them – ask for their names and addresses, and for a witness statement from each. As I pushed through them to reach the shop, I shouted that I wanted to interview them all very soon – and they began to wander away, but first I had to speak to Julie and Phyllida. I needed their account of things and fortunately both had remained in the shop; the owner, village butcher Arthur Drake, had also just arrived. Phyllida acted wisely and did the most sensible thing – she closed the door to prevent the public entering until I was satisfied they could do so without hampering the investigation, and then she made a cup of hot sweet tea for Julie and herself, the ideal comforter when in a state of shock. I could see that both were in a state of some shock which meant I had to be cautious and sensitive in the way I approached the formalities of the occasion.

Persuading witnesses to talk is often a good ploy, it helps to release tension and emotions, and so, before the chore of taking down written statements, I asked each of the women to provide me with a verbal account of their experience. The reality was, of course, that I needed as much information as I could obtain in the shortest possible time if I was to circulate a more detailed description of the wanted man.

Sadly, neither woman had seen much. Both had been at the far end of the counter, the part furthest away from the door and thus furthest away from the till, and they had been concentrating upon the finer points of a small joint of beef which Phyllida had been considering for her Sunday lunch.

Whilst their minds were focused upon the meat, the raider had rushed through the door which had been standing open at the time; the two women had glanced up only to see the man reach into the till which was perched on the end of the counter, grab a fistful of notes and race for the door. Julie had reacted with speed and bravery; she'd rushed along her side of the counter to try and stop the man but he'd thrown his free hand wide which had struck her on the side of the face, and then he was out of the shop, on his bike and heading towards Ashfordly. It was all over in seconds.

With Arthur Drake and Phyllida standing silently by, I began to quiz my first witness, Julie. Initially, she could not provide a very detailed description, but as I began to probe her memory, she recalled that the raider was a male about twenty-five, medium build with dark hair which was long and un-kempt, wearing motor cycling goggles, a white and red spotted duster around his mouth, and a brown leather jerkin. The goggles and duster, often worn by motor cyclists at that time, were an effective form of disguise because she had no clear idea of his facial features, neither did she know what kind of trousers or leggings he wore, nor the style or colour of his footwear. He had not spoken and so she did not know whether he was a local man or a visitor. To her recollection, she had not seen him before, either in the shop or elsewhere. She could offer no description of the motor bike – to her, it was merely a motor bike.

I asked Phyllida if she could add anything to Julie's account and she said she couldn't.

I got the impression that she hadn't seen anything at all and although I did question her briefly, she could add nothing to Julie's account. It was almost as if she hadn't realized what had happened, almost as if her mind was blank and I attributed it to the shock of the moment. Even without Phyllida's statement, there was enough detail for a fairly comprehensive description to be circulated, so, before settling down to gather the details for my written report, I went out to my van. I radioed a description of the motor cyclist to Control, for immediate circulation around the area and, after hearing how the thief had simply entered the shop, grabbed the cash and run out, I felt the presence of the Scenes of Crime team would be superfluous. The man had not left any fingerprints, footprints or other clues.

I had a quick word with Arthur but he had no idea who the culprit might be – he'd not sacked anyone recently, nor did he know of anyone with any kind of a grudge against him. From what I had learned, it appeared that the fellow was an opportunist, albeit one who must have seen the location of the till through the window at some earlier time. His rapid approach, and dash into the shop suggested he knew precisely where to direct his nefarious activities – but anyone looking into this shop window could see the till and it didn't require a genius to guess that its contents, late on a busy Saturday afternoon, would make easy and profitable picking. As a piece of crime prevention advice, I suggested that Arthur resite his till in a place less vulnerable to attack.

Then it was time to take the statements; these would be taken down in my official pocket book, in my own handwriting.

Each would be checked and signed by the

person making it. Then I would copy out each statement on my typewriter, with several carbon copies of each. Each statement would be attached to the crime report, one copy of which would find its way to Police Headquarters, one to Statistics Department, one to Divisional Headquarters, one to Sub-Divisional Headquarters and one for our file in Ashfordly and one for my own file at Aidensfield. It follows that incidents and reports of crime generated a lot of paperwork, much of which we had to administer ourselves.

There was a tiny office at the back of the shop. It contained a desk, a couple of chairs and a matching pair of four-drawer filing cabinets so I decided I would make use of it. Arthur gave his approval and I told him he could reopen the shop if he wished – but he declined, saying the shop closed at five anyway; it was already approaching five. I would take each witness in turn.

Arthur's statement was short and factual, a written record of the fact he knew of no suspects for the reasons he had already explained. I wrote it down in my book and he signed it. Julie's statement was equally easy to write down; she had a clear mind, she could describe events with clarity and ease, and although her contribution was quite lengthy, it was necessarily so because it contained a detailed description of the thief and a full account of the attack. Eventually, she agreed that everything she could recall had been included and signed my book. I said she was now free to go home if she wished, provided Arthur agreed – which he did.

Then it was the turn of Phyllida. I settled her down on one of the chairs, opened my book, made sure my ballpoint was flowing.

Although she had provided me with so little in the way of a verbal account, I felt that, having had time to settle down and gather her thoughts, she might recall something further and so I prepared to take down her statement, however brief it might be. I could see she was suddenly very nervous; she was clasping her hands across her lap to prevent them shaking and I saw her lick her lips once or twice. Then, speaking very quickly, she said, 'It's been a fortnight now, you know.'

'A fortnight?' I puzzled – and then I remembered a conversation we'd had some time ago. Phyllida had given up smoking! She'd told me all about it at the time, stressing how difficult it had been and what a battle of wills she had every time she smelt cigarette smoke.

'Two whole weeks, Mr Rhea, and never a one has crossed my lips. It's not easy, but I am determined not to start again.'

'Well done,' I praised her. 'You'll be much healthier now; smoking is never good for the health.'

'And they send their regards. They might be coming again – for a weekend, they said, when they rang last week. They might see you again, they asked me to tell you.'

'Did they?' Now tuned in to Phyllida's wavelength, I knew she was talking about her nephew and his wife who lived in Newcastle-on-Tyne. They were regular visitors to Aidensfield and sometimes I would join Jim, her nephew, for a drink in the pub – he was a policeman in Newcastle and we'd attended the same initial training course.

'I look forward to that.' I was sincere. Jim was good company and we got on very well indeed. 'But the statement, Phyllida...'

'I did tell Mrs Pinkerton what you said,' she went on. 'I think she was very pleased to get your advice and she's much happier now.'

'It's always nice to be able to help someone,' I smiled. 'It's all part of my job and I thought Mrs Pinkerton, being new as treasurer, was shy about asking about the rules relating to tombola and selling raffle tickets for the WI party...'

'She was so grateful,' beamed Phyllida. 'And you'll be pleased to know that I found it eventually. It was under the bed; it had fallen off the covers when I'd taken it off to wash my hands and it had somehow got kicked under there without me realizing.'

'Rings are easily lost about the house.' I recalled her reporting a family heirloom missing about two months earlier. 'I'm pleased you've found it, I'll cross it off our records now. I'm just pleased it wasn't stolen. Now, let's get this statement down...'

'Sorry, Mr Rhea, yes, we must get on. You are a busy man and I must not detain you with my tittle-tattle. What was it you wanted to talk to me about?'

'The snatch-thief,' I said. 'I just need a few words from you, written down in statement form; I'll record it in my notebook.'

'Why, what's happened?' she asked, her eyebrows furrowing in deep concentration.

'That's what I was hoping you'd tell me,' I smiled.

'Well, I have no idea what you are talking

90

about, Mr Rhea. Snatch-thief? What snatch-thief?'

'Just a few minutes ago, here in the shop ... the man with the motor bike...'

'What did he do?' and I could see the genuine puzzlement on her broad face. I knew that the effects of shock could do some funny things, but had it already wiped out her memory of such recent events?

'When you were talking to Julie about your Sunday joint, he rushed in and grabbed a fistful of money from the till...'

'Who did?' she asked.

'A man on a motor bike, he pulled up outside, left his engine running and dashed inside, grabbed the money and made good his escape. Julie saw him...'

'I don't know why you are asking me about it, Mr Rhea; you seem to know all about it. How should I know what happens in the shop? I don't live anywhere near it, I'm sorry, but I don't think I can help you.'

'No, I don't think you can,' I had to admit. 'But if you do think of anything when you get home, give me a ring. I'll come to see you later. Tomorrow perhaps?'

'Yes, you're more than welcome. But was it serious? I mean, was anyone hurt?'

'Not harmed, but Julie was very shocked...'

'Well, she would be if a man rushed in and stole money from right under her nose. I would be. I would be very shocked indeed. Have they arrested him then?'

'No, not yet. I need a description of him, you were in the shop, remember, when he came in.'

'Was I really?' There was a frown of disbelief on her face. 'I think you must be mistaken, PC Rhea. Perhaps it was someone else?'

I realized I was wasting my time and could only assume that, for reasons which may or may not be associated with the effects of shock, Phyllida had lost her memory of the incident, recent though it was. As a serving policeman, I had encountered amnesia on previous occasions, with people being unable to recall traffic accidents in which they had been involved, and others turning up in strange places and not knowing their own identity. Sometimes such losses of memory were restored with striking swiftness, occasionally resulting from a second severe shock or even a knock on the head ... but I had no intention of shocking Phyllida or knocking her on the head. I would have to be satisfied without her contribution to my statement file; if Phyllida could add so little to Julie's contribution, then her efforts would be futile.

I told the trio I had all the information I needed and that they could go home; I thanked them for their co-operation and said I would keep them informed about any developments, particularly if we traced the culprit. Then I left as they remained to chat a few moments with Arthur. I went home to ring the final details to Ashfordly Police Office; Alf Ventress, on duty in the office, would ensure that everything received immediate attention, that every patrolling officer knew about our raid and that they would look out for the thief and his motor bike, perhaps with visits to local pubs to see if anyone was being particularly generous with free drinks.

And tonight, before going off duty, I could compile my crime report. Before going home, however, I visited several houses and shops in the vicinity of the raided premises to ask whether the occupants had seen the crime, but none had. I asked them to let me know if they heard anyone claiming to have witnessed it and all promised their co-operation. I did pop into the post office for words with Oscar Blaketon, then the pub and the garage but found no one who had witnessed the raid.

Feeling that I had made very little progress I went home and after tea, I adjourned to my own office attached to the police house, and typed my report, along with copies of the statements I had obtained and details of the enquiries I had made around the village. As I finished this before nine o'clock and my shift was not due to end until ten, I decided to drive into Ashfordly to deliver my paperwork. When I arrived, Alf Ventress was in the enquiry office and Sergeant Craddock was in his own sanctum, completing some paperwork of his own, but he heard my arrival and came through to ask about progress. I explained what had happened and outlined my own subsequent actions whereupon he said,

'Well, PC Rhea, you've done all you can. Thank you for delivering the file so promptly. Good admin. is the sign of an efficient officer, you know, and I do like to get my paperwork completed in the shortest possible time.'

He asked Alf Ventress about his circulation of details of the raid, whereupon Alf reassured him that every possible avenue had been considered.

The control room at Force HQ had

radioed neighbouring forces, and Alf reiterated that every patrolling constable within fifty miles of Ashfordly had immediately been made aware of the bike, along with a description of its rider. 'They'd know within ten minutes of Nick informing me,' he told Craddock. 'We had a good description, but I think he'll have gone to ground by now.'

'You found some useful witnesses then?' Craddock put to me.

'The shop girl, Sergeant, Julie Weldon, and a customer, Phyllida Hobday.'

He had my file in his hands and flicked through it, nodding as he read Julie's statement, then he said, 'The assistant has done well, but there's nothing from the customer, PC Rhea, I thought you said she was a witness?'

'She was in the shop at the time, Sergeant, but can't recall seeing anything.'

'So she's not a witness, is she? If she did not see anything, maybe you should have obtained a negative statement?'

'She was actually in the shop, Sergeant, during the raid, and I think she did see something...'

'You mean she's shielding the culprit? She recognized him and is not revealing what she knows? She's not an accomplice, is she,

PC Rhea? Is that what you are trying to tell me?'

'No, I'm not saying that. There's no way she could be an accomplice...'

'Really, PC Rhea? And what makes you such a good judge of human nature? Good people do go off the rails, you know, for all sorts of reasons.'

'She's a very nice woman, Sergeant, she lives in the village and has done for years. She's a real good woman; she helps out with all the local groups and charities.'

'A saint, eh?'

'Look, Sergeant.' I began to get angry at his cynical response. 'I think she's lost her memory. I think the shock was such that it's affected her. I do know her well and would like to talk to her again, tomorrow perhaps or even later. When she's had time to compose herself.'

'Well, if she is in league with the thief, don't let her convince you she's all sweet-ness and light, PC Rhea. Be objective; don't be deflected from your duty, make sure her story tallies with that of the shop assistant...'

'Very good, Sergeant,' I said, and left him holding my crime report. I would go and have another word with Phyllida tomorrow – fortunately, it was a Sunday and so she would be at home. Having roast beef? I wondered if she'd actually secured the joint she'd been examining.

I rang the doorbell of her cottage about half-past eleven. She smiled and welcomed me, and I was admitted to her kitchen where a small joint was sitting in a roasting dish, awaiting its turn in the oven.

'Phyllida,' I said, 'it's about yesterday.'

'I was surprised how quickly he did it,' she said with conviction. 'It was the work of a moment...'

I wasn't sure whether she was talking about Arthur's skill in providing her with a suitably small joint of beef or something else – even the raider?

'Arthur, you mean?' I put to her. 'He is a master butcher, you know.'

'No, I mean that man on the motor bike. In and out like a flash he was, pushing that girl about. There's no manners these days, Mr Rhea, none at all.'

'You saw him?'

'Arthur? Yes, of course, I saw him, he came into the shop and made sure I had a very choice cut of best beef, Mr Rhea, such a nice man, he is.'

I had a feeling that this was not going to be easy. 'Can you describe the man on the bike?' I asked her slowly. 'Or even the bike?'

'Oh, yes, it was a BSA 350cc, Mr Rhea, with a black frame and a green petrol tank, I had a good look at it when the man was in the shop.'

'I don't suppose you saw the registration number?' I put to her. At that time, motor cycles carried two registration plates, one usually standing upright on the front mudguard so that it could be read from both sides, and the rear one flat against the rear mudguard.

'Oh, yes, I'm good at things like that, noticing details. It comes from working in a solicitor's office, you know. Yes, it was TUT. I remember that bit. TUT. And I saw the figures 3 and 7. I can't remember anything else though, because the man rushed out and rode off, didn't he? In a rush. There may have been more figures ... and I'm not sure of their order, but there was definitely a 3 and a 7, Mr Rhea.'

Wasting no time, I jotted down those details in my notebook and decided against asking her to make a formal written statement.

Feeling excited, I had the information I needed and was sure we could trace the machine and its rider or owner. I did quiz her a little more, but succeeded only in a statement that the sun had come out that day she'd seen me sheltering under the oak tree in Elsinby, and she'd been to the doctor to see about that business she'd mentioned at the village hall meeting. My immediate task was to trace the whereabout of any BSA 350cc motor bike with the registration letters TUT; the two final letters, UT, meant it was originally registered with Leicestershire County Council but if the owner now lived in the North Riding of Yorkshire, it might be recorded in our local vehicle taxation office in Grammar School Lane, Northallerton. Because it was a Sunday, it would be closed, but in cases of urgency, a constable from the town patrol could enter the premises and search the records. I thought my need was urgent, and so I hurried home, rang Northallerton and was told by the inspector that, without delay, he would dispatch an officer to make the necessary search. I had to wait near my phone from him to call back – it would take half an hour or so.

When the call came through, I learned that the BSA was owned by a youth called Edward George Cameron who lived in Ashfordly and so I drove into town for a quick word with Alf Ventress who knew everyone in the place. Sergeant Craddock was standing by as we talked.

'Ah, yes, young Cameron. He's been investing heavily on the horses in recent months,' Alf said. 'Never away from the betting shop, so I'm told. I did hear he'd got himself into debt.'

'I think it is time we paid him a visit, PC Rhea,' smiled Craddock.

Confronted by a pair of very stern looking police officers, Cameron readily admitted the crime, saying he'd been desperate for cash; we found about half of the takings in his bedroom but he'd spent the rest, paying off debts to his bookie. I arrested him and we took him to Ashfordly Police Station for due process and later, he was fined £50 and put on probation for three years.

'You did well, PC Rhea,' Craddock said when it was all over. 'That lady witness had a good memory for detail.'

'I think she functions a day later than most of us,' I smiled. 'But yes, in time she did produce the information we needed.'

'You'll say thank you to her, will you? On behalf of us all?'

'I will, Sergeant,' I assured him.

It would be a few days later when I saw

Phyllida walking towards the post office in Aidensfield and I hailed her.

'Ah, Phyllida,' I smiled. 'Just the lady! I want to thank you...'

'There were three of them last time I looked,' she smiled. 'One with dark-brown eyes and the others with long fluffy tails.'

'Really?' I said, but this time I had no idea what she was talking about.

Chapter 4

The story of the raid on Arthur Drake's shop came at a time which reminded me, and most of the Aidensfield folk, that Arthur owned a racehorse. Contrary to popular belief, Arthur was not a wealthy man, not a tycoon and owner of strings of racehorses; he was merely a village businessman in a very modest way. He owned a single shop in Aidensfield, he had a slaughterhouse at nearby Crampton and a couple of vans which toured the villages to provide a door-to-door service. He had acquired the horse as settlement for a substantial outstanding debt which had been long overdue. At the time, the horse had been a very insignificant animal, a foal born of a pair of unremarkable parents and Arthur thought he could keep her a while, then sell her to recoup the debt. Much to his surprise, however, the lovely filly had matured into a splendid animal and several local horserace enthusiasts had praised her apparent fitness while commenting upon her striking elegance.

One knowledgeable man from Elsinby, a village known for its wide-ranging horse-racing connections, had suggested that Arthur should have his horse professionally trained with a view to entering her at selected race meetings, starting very modestly with one or two local events. He'd expressed the view that the horse would easily cover its expenses and training fees, perhaps with a little profit for Arthur too.

Arthur knew a local trainer to whom he supplied meat and he struck a deal more as a kind of experiment than a real attempt at producing a winning racehorse. The outcome was that he suddenly and unexpectedly found himself with a very lively, responsive horse, and a potential race winner.

The trainer, with the unlikely name of Dick Rider, was very experienced and full of enthusiasm as he tried to impress upon Arthur that he really did have a very capable and exciting racehorse on his hands. Thus persuaded, Arthur began to consider a short term career for his filly; he had no desire to become a famous owner and I think his reason for proceeding in this way was to eventually sell the horse for rather more than he had earlier envisaged.

He called her Drake's Progress and the trainer began to quietly enter her at local flat meetings on courses at Catterick Bridge, Redcar, Thirsk, Thornaby, Beverley and Ripon. These were designed to familiarize the horse with the atmosphere of a race meeting rather than win outright at her first attempt, but they were a pointer to what the punters called 'form', and it seems the horse experienced no trouble settling into this new and exciting environment. She acquitted herself very well indeed – in fact, she was placed very frequently, she was third on more than one occasion and a creditable second on two outings. At the end of her first season, therefore, Drake's Progress had begun to make an impact and people were beginning to talk about Arthur's handsome filly. Arthur, however, did not boast about his horse – I think he was bemused by the entire affair, having found himself owning something unexpectedly successful.

The following year, Drake's Progress was entered for some early races in the new flat season and although I was not a racing fan, I did witness her successes at several tracks, simply because I happened to be on duty on the tracks in question. Racecourse duty was one of our more pleasant commitments.

We policed all the meetings within the North Riding of Yorkshire, and, through a freak of geography, York Races. The chief task for most of the uniformed officers was to ensure the orderly parking of cars and coaches prior to the first race, and then we adjourned to one or other of the enclosures to join our other colleagues, ostensibly to keep public order, prevent drunkenness, deter criminals and pickpockets and generally ensure a peaceful meeting. For many of us, particularly the young constables, it was an introduction to a way of life we could never achieve – we drooled over Rolls-Royce cars in the posh car parks, especially those with picnic hampers and champagne in the boots; we admired the smart sports cars and the lovely women they seemed to attract and we patrolled the expensive rings, trying to understand racing terms, tick-tack men and betting odds. Sometimes, if we could find one of our plain clothes officers, or perhaps a good friend, we would ask them to place a modest bet for us, either on the Tote or with a reputable bookmaker. We were not allowed to place bets whilst in uniform, nor could we sip pints at the bars or take part in any of the festivities. We were police officers and we were on duty to uphold the law and keep the peace – that was our job and there were senior officers on the course to supervise us. Furthermore, some of our very senior officers were racing fans and could be expected to attend – and so, being constantly in the public eye, we had to be sure we were always on our best behaviour.

And so it was that I found myself attending the April meeting at Catterick Bridge along with a posse of my colleagues. I was on car-parking duty prior to the first race and then I had to patrol Tattersalls until the start of the last race.

As everyone was preparing for the last race I had to adjourn, with my colleagues, to the car-park to help the cars depart. At that time, the Great North Road (the Al), ran directly past the racecourse, consequently race traffic leaving the car parks had to be carefully controlled and supervised to prevent accidents and hold-ups.

Catterick Bridge is a very small and attractive course, known locally as the Farmers' Racecourse. It dates from the seventeenth century and for the first hundred years or more, it functioned on a very modest income, with some expenses being incurred for tar and feathers which were used to punish 'welshers' – dishonest bookies who were then thrown into the nearby River Swale. Private horserace contests would sometimes be held here, with prizes of a bottle of wine or port. Throughout its history, Catterick's modest track has attracted farmers from the Yorkshire Dales and south Durham – which might explain why there was no entrance charge in its early days – and it is known for both the sporting attitude of its supporters and managers, and their ability to improvise. There was one famous occasion in winter, with National Hunt racing on the agenda, when the course was covered with thick snow which, in most cases, would have caused a race meeting to be abandoned. But not at Catterick Bridge! The owner of the nearby Bridge Hotel, called Thomas Ferguson (owner of the 1819 St Leger winner, Antonio) gathered together a large flock of sheep and drove them round and round the course until every flake of snow had been cleared. Thanks to his actions, the meeting went ahead.

At the April meeting in question, however, I had completed my car-parking chores and crossed the busy road towards Tattersalls where I was to be on duty for the duration of the meeting, i.e. until just before the last race. I bought myself a race card so that I could follow the proceedings and even have a little bet if I found a horse I fancied. Being very inexperienced at understanding the horse-racing world, I chatted with a colleague called Colin and we decided to invest a pound each on the Tote Double. The Double was based on the second race and the fifth; the idea was that we placed a bet on a horse running in the second race and if that won, we would put the winnings on a horse in the fifth. As Colin had no idea what to do either, we looked at the list of runners for the second race and I was pleasantly surprised to find Drake's Progress listed as No.2 on the card. That news had not permeated into Aidensfield, but when I checked the betting, the filly was shown as 8 to 1, by no means the favourite. Nonetheless, I felt I should invest my modest £1 on Arthur's horse. I felt he would be here to see his horse run, but hadn't come across him and so I could not seek his advice about the true merits of his investment.

Colin said that if I was backing Drakes's Progress, then he would do likewise. After the first race, therefore, we found a detective friend and asked him to place our bets with the Tote – a pound win for each of us. Much to our surprise, Drake's Progress won by a clear length. We were rich – well, richer is perhaps the right term, but our winnings now had to be placed on something running in the fifth race. We did not place a bet on the interim races, being too preoccupied in finding a suitable candidate in the fifth.

Picking a winner, when one is totally ignorant of the skills required to become a successful punter, is little more than a lottery, and then I spotted a horse in the fifth which bore the name Golden Hind. I knew that was the name of the ship which carried Sir Francis Drake on his voyages of discovery. My thoughts immediately linked Sir Francis and Arthur – two Drakes! Thinking that fortune often favoured such unlikely paths (and having once won a few bob by betting on horses, jockeys and trainers who bore the names of birds), I settled for Golden Hind as my Tote Double choice. Colin said he would do likewise, but I suggested we find another horse for him, so that our bets would be spread across a wider net. He agreed, and found one called Pelican Crossing – he thought the daft link between a drake and a pelican was sufficient to convince him. I explained I'd successfully executed a similar coup in the past based on such illogicalities, and so we decided to proceed. Golden Hind was No.2 on the race card, Pelican Crossing was No.9. We found a mutual friend, another detective in civilian clothes, and asked him to place our bets for us – No.2 and No.9 in the fifth race.

Unfortunately, in the noise of the course, the clerk at the Tote window misheard him. When he said 'Two and Nine please,' she had thought he'd said 'Two number nine' and so he came away with two tickets for No.9 – Pelican Crossing. And the odds for it were 12 to 1, by no means a favourite. Our friend had no idea he had received the wrong one on our behalf and in retrospect, we could have changed the tickets, I am sure, but at the time, and with the race about to start, we decided to keep them.

Pelican Crossing won. In something of a daze, we collected our Tote winnings which came to £185 – more than £90 each. More than a month's wages for poor constables!

Sitting in the personnel carrier on the way home after the meeting, we discussed our lucky streak, with Colin saying, 'I'm chuffed to bits we went for the bird theme instead of relying on the sailing connections...'

'Don't be daft,' said the voice of another

colleague. 'You stuck to Drake all along ... the *Golden Hind* was called *Pelican* before it changed its name ... *Golden Hind* was its second name.'

But that little outing persuaded me that betting in such a bizarre manner is often as good as spending hours studying form, only to lose by the shortest of heads.

This was just one example when the people of Aidensfield began to feel a deep sense of pride at having a successful race-horse which was so closely associated with the village. Each time it appeared, therefore, many of them would back Drake's Progress and some would even travel to the course where she was running. Bernie Scripps managed to organize supporters' coach parties from time to time, thanks to co-operation from Arnold Merryweather and his bus company, while Claude Jeremiah Greengrass earned himself a few pounds by becoming a bookie's runner. Even if he conducted his business in the pub, he kept his activities sheltered from the eagle eyes of the law – myself included (although, in these rather special circumstances, I might have turned a blind eye to such minor illegalities). After all, Arthur's horse was good for the economy of Aidensfield.

Later, we were all delighted when we learned that Drake's Progress was to run in the Crampton Stakes at the Ebor Meeting on York's renowned Knavesmire. She wasn't entered in the Ebor Handicap itself, but in the third race on the final day of that annual August meeting – the Ascot of the North. To win the Crampton Stakes, with more than £12,000 prize money, would be a true accolade for Arthur's wonder horse. This time, the impending event generated something akin to the atmosphere of a coronation or royal visit in Aidensfield, because the people began to talk about street parties, bunting upon the houses, coloured lights and bonfires, barbecues and roast oxen, a dance in the village hall and even the planting of a celebratory oak tree. Bus trips were to be organized to York Races too, courtesy of Arnold Merryweather, the idea being that anyone wishing to attend could do so, and that the use of coaches would eliminate worries about drinking and driving. The next thing I knew was that a committee had been formed to make the necessary arrangements. The planned Drake's Progress party would be on the Thursday of Ebor week, the day the horse was to run while carrying the hopes – and cash – of most of the villagers. I was asked to join the committee to advise on any legal matters which might arise, such as drinking alcohol in the street and in the village hall, arranging tombolas and raffles, making sure the young people were catered for, and, of course, car-parking and other practicalities involving large numbers of people assembled in one place. It was even suggested that Drakes' Progress herself might make a guest appearance, perhaps to draw the raffle or to make some other gesture – that depended upon the trainer's advice.

Someone suggested an official shovel might be a sensible idea too, while Claude Jeremiah Greengrass suggested the raffling of any deposits the horse might make because droppings were very good for rose bushes, although another committee member felt it might be better used for nourishing the suggested oak tree.

News of the planning arrangements soon reached the ears of Sergeant Craddock at Ashfordly Police Station. When I popped into the office one morning to deliver some reports, he hailed me.

'PC Rhea, a word if I may.'

'Sergeant?'

'I have received an application from your

local landlord, George Ward at the Brewers' Arms in Aidensfield. For a Special Order of Exemption and an Occasional Licence, both on the same day. The first is for his premises, wanting to extend licensing hours until one o'clock, and the Occasional Licence is for the village hall, from eight until midnight on the same day. Those two facts, added together, seem to suggest some kind of almighty booze-up, if I am not mistaken. He does go on to say, though, that there is a special occasion that day – a vital ingredient of the former licence is the need for some very special occasion, I might add – but he says that the occasion is York Races. Now, PC Rhea, Aidensfield is a long way from York, and I can't think the races are special to Aidensfield – I mean, they occur year in and year out, and they feature a good number of racing days. So, tell me, what is so special in Aidensfield about that race meeting in York?'

'It's not the races that are special, Sergeant, it's the fact that a local horse is running that day. I did ask George to make that clear in his application.'

'Ah, a local horse! And why is that so special?'

I explained how Arthur had acquired the

foal and how it had blossomed, like the ugly duckling turning into a swan. I must admit I glamorized my account to some degree, adding that the success of the horse had generated a wonderfully festive atmosphere in Aidensfield, and that I believed the occasion was very special indeed, certainly worthy of a full-blooded celebration – properly conducted, of course.

'And the people are placing bets on the horse, are they?' he asked.

'Yes, some have already done so early, to get better odds, but I do know that most of the village will be backing her; there are bus trips to York too, to watch the race.'

'I do hope there will be no illegal betting in your village, PC Rhea,' he said. 'You will be keeping an eye on that man Greengrass, I trust, and his activities in licensed premises so far as betting is concerned.'

'I've already spoken to him, Sergeant,' I assured him.

'Good, well, in the circumstances, I cannot see that we can raise any objection to these applications, even if I do not understand the fuss about a horse running against other horses. I am not a betting man, PC Rhea, my Welsh chapel upbringing you understand, but I am sufficiently open-minded not to object to those who do. I have sufficient faith in you to keep things under control in Aidensfield on that occasion, and so I shall not object to either of these applications.'

'Thank you, Sergeant.'

'I shall present them to the magistrates at the next petty sessions,' he said. 'But I see no problem. Now, what did you say that horse was called?'

'Drake's Progress,' I said. 'It is owned by our butcher, Arthur Drake.'

'Good, thank you. I shall make a note of that. For the official record, you understand.'

'Of course, Sergeant.'

Had Drake's Progress been running in the Grand National, I doubt if there would have been as much enthusiasm and interest, and the village produced a wonderful party to celebrate. Being August, a barbecue had been planned on the village green, the streets were decorated with flowers, bunting and lights which would be switched on at dusk, a dance had been arranged in the village hall, with a bar and the pub was granted its extension of hours. Four coach-loads of supporters were assembled outside the church on the morning of the race meeting, but I was already there – I was on duty at York Races that day, but my duties finished with the emptying of the car-parks on the Thursday. I would be back in Aidensfield in time for the celebrations – but then, I would be off duty. Phil Bellamy had been drafted in to take my place on a late patrol of Aidensfield, Ashfordly and district, and so I could relax. Like all the other villagers, I had placed my bet on Drake's Progress some time ahead of the race meeting, and had secured good odds of 7 to 1 – and with five pounds riding on her back, I had reason to celebrate if she won. *When* she won!

I must admit there was a feeling in the village that Drake's Progress could not lose – she had had a hugely successful season up to that point, with three wins, two seconds and a third: a good record. In the week before the race, Arthur had vanished from his usual haunts, taking a break in a York hotel to be close to the course for the entire Ebor Meeting, but away from those who persistently tried to abstract the tiniest details of extra information about his horse. On that Thursday, my duties were as usual – car-parking prior to the first race, Tattersalls during the racing, and traffic control after the start of the last race. But I would see the races and I would be able to watch Drake's Progress, along with about 200 Aidens-fielders, and I would be home in time for the celebrations.

'But what if she loses?' one of my colleagues said to me as I told him about the Aidensfield horse.

'Drake's Progress won't lose!' I must have said that hundreds of times, but the possibility niggled at me. What on earth would we celebrate tonight if Drake's Progress did not win? I could understand Arthur wanting to keep out of the way, but there were all those Aidensfield folk on the course right now...

The hours before racing kept me very busy – car-parking in those days was a hectic business, with so many motorists wanting to do something which would disrupt the whole system and it was not easy maintaining a calm approach in the face of smart-accented hostility, but in time, all the cars were parked in an orderly manner and all would be able to leave smoothly afterwards.

I went into the course, found myself a race-card, and settled down to regular patrols in between the races, and managing to secure a few bets as well. I did see many of the Aidensfield party, spread out across different parts of the course, and I could see that all were eagerly awaiting the great moment. And then the runners were called; I heard the voice saying, 'Weighed in' and it was almost time for the Crampton Stakes. I watched the bookies chalking up the odds for the runners, I listened to the Tannoy; scanned the Tote information boards and then the horses were trotting up to the start. I found Drake's Progress, with her jockey in her colours of bottle green and brown, and she seemed to be relishing the atmosphere of the racecourse. I found myself easing towards the rails so that I could have a good view of the finish, and saw the faces of friends and Aidensfielders all around me, and then the horses were lined up for the start.

It was a seven furlong race with twelve runners and Drake's Progress was second favourite with odds of 2 to 1, and then they were off. I knew the race would last for a very short time but it all happened so quickly ... almost before I realized, the field was thundering towards the finishing post and I saw Drake's Progress neck and neck with two other horses. The shouting of the jockeys, the noise of the crowd and the thunder of the horses' hooves on the turf was dramatic in the extreme and I found myself standing there and shouting as I waved my arms and called the name of Drake's Progress. As they crossed the finishing line, I realized where I was ... I had no idea which horse had won then a voice said, 'Photo' and I looked around, embarrassed by my loss of control whilst in uniform.

But no one seemed to have noticed – everyone was too busy cheering on the horses and trying to see which had won. I walked away and as I turned from my place, I saw Sergeant Craddock, in civilian clothes, with a big smile on his face.

'Sergeant!' I said. 'Fancy seeing you here...'

'I thought I might come to see what the fuss was all about.' He looked slightly embarrassed. 'Very exciting, though, I must admit. Very exciting indeed.'

'Who won?' I asked.

'I've no idea,' He shook his head. 'Three of them crossed the line together, neck and neck it was.'

'And Drake's Progress?'

'She was with them. I do hope she won,

you know, er, I got PC Ventress to place a modest bet on her for me, he knows about these things ... well, once I hear the result, I must get away before the traffic builds up...'

'You'll be coming to Aidensfield tonight?' I put to him.

'No, I think not, PC Rhea. You do not want your sergeant breathing down your neck on such an occasion. No, I shall take my wife dancing, we belong to a club in Ashfordly.'

And he vanished into the crowd. It was an agonizing wait as I joined some of my colleagues, and then came the result. A dead heat for first place. Most unusual ... and Drake's Progress was one of the two in question. The third horse had been half a head behind. So Drake's Progress did win.

I collected my winnings and there were celebrations in Aidensfield that night.

Arthur received a whopping offer for Drake's Progress and within a couple of months, he had sold her. She continued to win races but somehow, there was not the interest in Aidensfield.

However, she attended our celebrations, and drew the raffle, (with a little help from Arthur) and she fertilized a nice oak tree which was planted outside the butcher's shop to her memory. It continues to make very good progress.

The achievements of Drake's Progress were not the only sporting highlights to generate widespread interest in Aidensfield during my time as the village constable. Apart from dramas affecting the cricket team, men's and women's tennis teams, pub darts and domino teams, and the two football teams (senior and junior), the village had resurrected its tug-of-war skills. It must be said that most, if not all, the Aidensfield residents had forgotten all about the annual tug-of-war contest between Aidensfield and Crampton, but it was Claude Jeremiah Greengrass who spotted an article about it in an old book among some other items he bought at a farm sale. At that time, the contest was held every year on the first Saturday in July, the trophy being a miniature replica of a half barrel containing models of loaves. It could be seen in the parish church of either Aidensfield or Crampton but no one seemed to know if it was still on display. We could check with the vicars.

The book *A History of the Parish of Aidensfield,* by A Resident, which had been published in 1835, gave a wonderful account of the growth of the village from its earliest days, and included details of many of its customs.

One was the use of the village green as a golf course, and another being the annual tug-of-war between teams from Aidensfield and Crampton. The tug-of-war was still being contested in 1835, the year the book had been published, but not even the oldest resident could recall it happening within living memory. I was in the pub, off duty one evening, when Claude arrived clutching his precious book and he regaled the regulars with the history of the tug-of-war. It seemed that, in the dim and distant past, the villages of Crampton and Aidensfield, with others nearby, had been suffering from a terrible famine and dreadful floods. At the height of the disaster, an Aidensfield resident had spotted, bobbing along in the flood water, what appeared to be the bottom half of a large wooden barrel. It was full of loaves and had apparently been washed away from a flooded bakery somewhere upriver. At almost the same moment, a resident of Crampton also spotted it, but neither could reach it or retrieve it. It sailed along the middle of the flooded river which marked the boundary between the two villages and as they watched, it came to rest in the hollow face of a boulder right in the middle of the flooded river. The power of the rushing water held the barrel in place, but equally, the depth and ferocity of it prevented people wading across to retrieve the goodies. There was a primitive bridge about quarter of a mile downstream, but its presence did not help the situation. You could not reach the barrel from the safety of that bridge. The barrel, which had two metal handles on the outer portion, contained sufficient bread to enable all the people of either Aidensfield or Crampton to survive a week more and so, once news of its presence reached the elders, it was decided to find a way of retrieving the loaves.

The Aidensfielders hit upon the idea of using a large metal hook at the end of a long rope, rather like a grappling iron. It would be tossed across to the barrel in the hope it would lodge with its point inside one of the handles so that the barrel could be hauled towards the shore. It would have to be done most carefully and without toppling the contents into the water. Living in the community were expert tossers of horseshoes (a sport which developed into the game of quoits) and skilled users of ropes for lassooing cattle and horses. It was felt that a person with these skills could effect a rescue.

The problem was that the people of Crampton had the same idea. Within each opposing village, therefore, there developed a race to find a man capable of securing the barrel, plus finding a length of rope with a hook on the end which was long enough to achieve that purpose. As word of the treasure trove spread around, so hungry people began to gather on the banks of the river and, eventually, the two champions arrived, one at each side of the flooded river. Each had produced the necessary length of rope with a solid hook on the end. They began to throw their hooks towards the barrel, sometimes missing altogether and sometimes narrowly failing to lodge the point of the hook inside the nearest handle – and then came success! The Aidensfield man secured a connection – as his hook slid into place, his supporters cheered and he tugged the rope gently to test its effect and then began the tricky task of dislodging the barrel in the force of the roaring water and towing it ashore without upskittling it. But even as he began his operation, the Crampton champion did likewise.

His hook lodged securely in place and he began his attempt to tow the barrel to his side of the river.

And thus a tug-of-war began.

As each man tugged in the hope he could overpower his rival while securing the bread, so more villagers came forward to seize their ropes and lend their strength to aid their champion. The ropes were long enough to permit nine people at each side and so began a mammoth tug-of-war with the bread as a prize. It is not recorded how long the people of each village tried desperately to haul the lifesaving bread to their own side of the river, but eventually, the inevitable happened. With the weight of two teams hauling upon the wooden panels of the barrel, the hooks were pulled off – along with the panels to which they were attached; flood water rushed in, the barrel overturned and dozens of loaves of bread tumbled into the river. They were whisked away upon the floodwater, never to be seen again. Several people tried to wade into the river in the hope of catching at least one loaf, but it was too deep and the current too powerful. Every scrap of bread was destroyed, and the barrel was smashed into smithereens by the pounding of the water;

broken into several pieces, it vanished forever. Neither side achieved anything by their efforts.

There were recriminations, of course, with the parish priests of each village denouncing the attempt as a demonstration of greed by both sides. 'If you had helped each other instead of pulling in opposite directions, you would have both had bread,' they had said to their congregations at mass the following Sunday.

As a result, and as a reminder of their folly, the actions of each village were commemorated in an annual tug-of-war contest. The actual site of that original battle was used, for the large central rock remained over the centuries and marked the precise middle of the river, even when not in flood. For the contest, teams of nine men from each village took part, with the middle of the rope being marked with a white rag; this marker had to be positioned precisely over the top of the famous rock before the match began. On the command 'Ready, steady, pull' therefore, each team had to try and drag the opposition into the water – the first team to put a foot into the edge of the river was the loser. The trophy, a replica of the half-barrel of bread, remained within the parish church of either Crampton or Aidensfield; it was accompanied by an account of its history but it was transferred between each church every alternate year, irrespective of who won the tug-of-war. It seems that neither team liked to be associated with that first very ancient fiasco and so the trophy remained within the churches as a reminder of their ancient folly – and over the years, the topic provided inspiration for many a sermon. With the passage of time, however, the tug-of-war had become little more than a sporting contest with few people recalling its origins, but even as a mere sporting challenge, it had come to an end at some unknown date in the past.

'I think we should resurrect it,' said Claude. 'It could be part of our summer sports day or garden fête or something.'

'What's in it for you, Claude?' asked Oscar Blaketon, ever sceptical about Claude's schemes. Blaketon was now one of the regulars at the bar, having retired from the police to run the local post office. In this capacity, I came into contact with him from time to time; now, we were enjoying a drink together in our local bar.

'Me? Nowt?' snorted Greengrass. 'Not

unless you want to buy a good long rope. I might be able to put my hands on one, at a fair price, a special with tug-of-war strength and a good grip.'

'You wouldn't be thinking of running a book on it, would you?' smirked Blaketon. 'Being a bookie's runner in the pub or something similarly illegal and dodgy? Like finding some other scam to make yourself a bit of tax-free loot?'

'Look, all I did was find this book with a bit of our history in it, and because I respect our past, I think we might revive it...'

'I could sponsor it,' beamed George, the landlord. 'Or mebbe get my brewery to sponsor it, with T-shirts carrying the pub name or summat. There's no pub in Crampton, so they'd have to find somebody else as their sponsor, Lord Crampton mebbe. He's into horseracing and other things so he might cough up a few quid for some shirts.'

As this chatter continued, other regulars joined in and it became quite evident that there was some enthusiasm for a revival of the tug-of-war competition, at least in Aidensfield. No one, at this early stage, had discussed the matter with the people of Crampton, but when a retired history teacher, then living in Crampton, heard about it, he thought it was a wonderful idea.

He began to make overtures around Crampton to seek views from the local people and before we realized it, a committee had been formed and it had been decided the forthcoming summer should witness the restoration of the historic tug-of-war contest. The ancient trophy would not be reallocated however; it would continue to alternate between the two churches but a new, more modern reward, not linked in any way to the bread of the past, would be created. A simple silver-coloured cup on a black plinth would be awarded to the winning team, and George Ward said he would also provide three free pints to each of the winners on the night of the contest. 'They'll pull the rope and I'll pull the pints,' he said.

In an attempt to be impartial, the tug-of-war would not be part of any other function in either Aidensfield or Crampton, and would therefore stand on its own merits. It would take place at the historic site of that very first tug with the rock marking the centre of the river; spectators could assemble along the river-banks, there would be a collection for local charities and there was also a good vantage point from the bridge which had been built over the river in the nineteenth century. I had little part in the preparatory arrangements, other than to be aware of the event although I do know that Claude, when there was no police around, *was* busy running a book on the outcome.

Claude produced a long length of rope, volunteers put their names forward as team members and there were rehearsals in a field behind the pub, with the eventual idea of selecting the final nine. A referee was eventually appointed, a headmaster who lived at Elsinby; he would be independent.

Some three weeks before the great day, both the Crampton and Aidensfield teams had made their final selections of competitors, each with three reserves, and the teams settled down to their earnest training. Whenever I patrolled past the pub, there they were, straining against the rope and leaning their weight upon it as they endeavoured not to give way, not to let their feet move and relying on their anchor man to hold firm. At one point, they even hitched their rope to a tractor and tried to prevent it moving away ... and, much to my surprise, the Aidensfield anchor man was none other than Claude Jeremiah Greengrass.

When I expressed my surprise at his choice, he grinned and said, 'There's nowt to it, Constable Nick, I wrap the end round my shoulders, you do it in a special way, then I hang on to it and dig my heels in ... that's all. Just hang on there ... lean back into it, in a manner of speaking...'

A week or so before the contest, I decided to inspect the site so that I knew precisely where it was going to occur; I needed to be prepared for any emergency – like knowing the best way to get a vehicle, such as an ambulance, down to the river if necessary. I found the spot – the large rock in the middle of the river was unmistakable, looking almost like an island as the summer water level was quite low, and the riverbanks were quite low too. People would not be dragged over cliffs or fall off them into the water – even though the banks were overgrown with trees, there was grass beneath which sloped gently into the water. The water was shallow at the edges and I could not see any risks here, other than a good soaking.

The crowds could not get very close to the competitors – the dense trees prevented that – but they could stand high on the river banks at either side, or the bridge. I wondered how the umpire could operate. From the bridge, I guessed, because he could not stand on both sides of the river simultaneously. And, on looking closely at the site, there was not a great deal of space on either side of the river for the teams – but I was sure they had taken all such matters into account.

On the day, things had been finalized as they tend to be and the umpire had appointed a couple of referees, one to stand at each side of the river while he stood on the bridge to oversee events. The two teams each gathered at their own side of the water, flexing their muscles and shouting rude remarks at the opposition while a goodly crowd assembled on whatever vantage points they could find. I stood back from the more dense parts of the crowd, and then all was ready. It had been decided that the contest would be the best of three pulls, the losers being the first team to have three or more people with feet in the river.

The rope had been cast across the water; each referee seized his respective section and hauled it until the rope was slung above the river and the white marker was central over the middle rock. The teams took their sections next, each gripping the rope and holding it taut, and then the umpire blew a whistle and called, 'Take the weight...'

The tug-of-war teams leaned backwards now, the rope became very taut across the water, and I saw each man dig in his heels lean further back with the rope tucked tight under their right armpits and their hands gripping the body of the rope.

I could see that Greengrass, standing very close to a small larch tree, had wrapped his tail end of rope around one shoulder and he was holding the loose end ... his heels were dug in too, gaining vital traction in the soft earth and the roots of alders and larches which riddled the ground at this point. Larches are known for their shallow roots and some were protruding at this point, providing extra anchorage for some boots.

'Take the strain,' called the umpire, then he paused and shouted, 'Ready, steady – pull!'

The crowd began to shout encouragement as the teams took the immense strain. Standing at the Aidensfield side of the river, I could see that the lead members were struggling to keep their feet. But the rear members held firm and with each team giving a few inches and then recovering those inches and more, it seemed that

135

neither would give way – and then Crampton lost their hold. Suddenly, the Aidensfield end of the rope moved about a yard and we saw the first splashes of water from the far side. A whistle blew – Aidensfield had won the first round.

Cheers filled the air as the teams relaxed for five minutes. Boots were cleaned of surplus mud, new footholds were found, a few team members changed position and then the whistle blew for the second round. It was a repetition of the first, but this time Crampton won; it was a long, hard tussle but they succeeded in pulling the required three Aidensfielders into the water. One all.

Now for the final pull.

The teams were given a further five minutes' relaxation as they made their preparations, spitting on their hands, digging in their heels and taking deep breaths for this critical pull. The umpire called for them to prepare, waited and then gave the order to pull – 'Ready, steady – pull!'

The roars of encouragement from the supporters were deafening, and I could see the strain on the faces of the team members as they gave everything in that final pull. On this occasion, Aidensfield seemed to be the more dominant, they were not giving, their feet seemed to be planted deep in the earth and their faces revealed the determination they were exerting. Then something happened – they seemed to give a little – but to give even the tiniest fraction in a competition of this kind can be critical and I could hear the increasingly excited shouts from the far side of the water. Crampton seemed to be winning; I saw the lead Aidensfield man slip a fraction, he was having trouble keeping his feet on their spot and I thought his knees were beginning to buckle ... everyone was shouting, the teams were perspiring and then ... calamity.

A riverside larch tree began to move. It looked half dead and its leafless branches above the team signalled that it was unstable; it was immediately behind Claude Jeremiah. Someone shouted a warning. It was falling and the Aidensfield team dropped their rope just in time and fled as the thirty-foot tree toppled onto the very spot where they had been standing – and at the far side of the river, all members of the Crampton team were lying flat on their backs, thrown over by the sudden release of tension.

The tree crashed to earth with its uppermost branches lying in the water and almost reaching the middle rock as the Aidensfield team members gathered their wits and scrambled to their feet. The referee blew his whistle and called for the umpire. The end of the Aidensfield rope had been tied around the trunk of that tree ... it was clearly visible now.

'Mr Greengrass?' demanded the umpire when he arrived. 'Might I ask you how this could have happened? Your end of the rope is around that tree trunk as well as being around you ... I do know you were standing rather close to it ... this is cheating, Mr Greengrass. I declare this contest null and void. I shall report to your committee and make recommendations...' And he stormed off, as if he had suffered some personal insult.

A sullen silence now fell upon the scene with Greengrass looking like his dog Alfred when caught stealing sausages; then George Ward said, 'Claude is buying the drinks, all tonight, lads.'

'Me? But they won, didn't they? Crampton, I mean. They won anyway...' he grunted. 'I don't see why I should—'

'Claude, you are buying drinks tonight,' said George. 'You cheated, which means *we* cheated, *Aidensfield* cheated ... that is terrible...'

'Aye, well, I mean, it's not that I'm a very good anchor man ... that tree looked sound enough to me ... how was I to know it was rotten?'

'Rotten like you, Claude!' snapped someone.

No one seemed inclined to consider a re-run of the contest and no one raised the question of continuing it next year. I think the Aidensfield-Crampton tug-of-war was destined to become an event with which no one wanted to be associated.

Chapter 5

When the telephone rang in my office just after 8.30 one Friday morning, I thought it was an emergency of some kind. It wasn't often it rang at that time – if Sergeant Craddock or anyone at Divisional HQ wanted to contact me, they would wait until nine. I made a habit of being in my office between nine and ten on most of the days I was on duty, and I made sure the local people knew that. For emergencies, of course, they could always dial 999 if it was very urgent, or ring one of the fully manned police stations in which case I would be contacted by radio if I was not at home. Failing that, Mary, my wife – and unpaid assistant – might be at home in which case she could make sure any messages reached me whilst I was on patrol. So, for all sorts of minor reasons, this call's timing was rather unusual.

'PC Rhea, Aidensfield,' I announced.

'Ah, Constable.' The accent told me this was not a local person; it sounded like an official from Buckingham Palace or a shop assistant from Harrods. 'I am not sure whether it is you I should be speaking to, or someone in higher authority. I rang you because you are the local constable, so perhaps you could advise me?'

'Yes, sir, of course,' I responded. 'If you could explain your requirements, I will help all I can.'

'Splendid fellow. I need a smart officer for an hour or so, to do traffic duty in this village.'

'Which village is that, sir?' I asked.

'Gelderslack. My name is Sir Giles Pifflington of Gelderslack House, by the way, a good friend of the Chief Constable as I am sure you realize.'

'And how can we help, Sir Giles?' I asked, ignoring his claims to friends in high places. There were times I felt the chief constable had more friends than he realized, most of whom seemed to want something rather special upon the strength of it. I had come across Sir Giles from time to time, recognizing him at various important functions in the district, although I had never been to his splendid, if rather isolated, mansion. He was a tall slender man who dressed impeccably in smart dark suits, white shirts and brightly polished black shoes with toe caps. With a small rounded head and sleek black hair, he looked as if he might wear a monocle, although I'd never seen him sporting one. In private perhaps?

'It is a family funeral, Constable,' he explained. 'I feel a constable is necessary to control traffic, particularly as my drive leads directly on to the main road.'

'Well, yes, that should be no problem at all, sir,' I assured him.

In rural areas, this kind of duty was quite normal. If there was a special event of any kind – wedding, funeral, harvest festival, village show, a garden fête or anything which generated extra traffic or crowds, then we would attend so that the minimum of congestion occurred. With traffic, of course, especially where the main roads were involved, our primary concern was for the safety of everyone. Our efforts to this end were especially appreciated at weddings and funerals where it was so important that the VIP vehicles were not hindered at or near the church or graveyard.

Even when safety was not the primary factor, such tasks were always a very good police/public relations exercise.

'So when would you require the constable?' I asked him.

'I'm afraid it is rather short notice,' he apologised. 'But it is being held tomorrow afternoon, Saturday. We leave the house at three.'

'Ah!' I breathed. 'Normally, I would have agreed to come along but I am scheduled for town duty in Ashfordly tomorrow afternoon. But leave it with me, Sir Giles, and I will speak to my sergeant. I'm not totally sure of our precise commitments at that time, but I'm sure something can be arranged. If I cannot attend, then I'm sure we will make someone available. I'll call you back very shortly.'

'Good man,' he said, and replaced his phone.

My duty rota showed that I was to perform a four-hour patrol in Ashfordly on Saturday, from two in the afternoon until six in the evening and, as I pondered that commitment, I remembered my presence was required because it was Ashfordly Show day. As always, a large crowd was expected and all available officers had been drafted in for a range of duties. I was to patrol Ashfordly town centre, with particular attention to the junction of two main roads which would become congested with show traffic unless the flow of vehicles was carefully controlled and monitored. In the realization of those commitments, I began to have doubts whether we could spare a constable for Sir Giles Pifflington's family funeral; after all, such a matter, in a fairly remote and quiet moorland village, was of low priority even if the drive of his house did emerge on to a main road. It was the sort of duty we would perform if there was nothing else of greater importance to concern us; nonetheless, I decided to call Sergeant Craddock.

'What's the matter, PC Rhea? Can't you sleep? I have not yet reached the office, I am still in my house and I haven't even got my tie on.'

'It is after half past eight,' I responded.

'So what's the problem?' he almost spat into the phone.

'I've had a call from a man on my beat, Sergeant, he wants me to perform traffic duty at a family funeral, tomorrow afternoon. The cortège leaves the house at three.'

'Tomorrow? But it's Ashfordly Show day, we need every available constable in town, otherwise heavy traffic will bring the place to a standstill, PC Rhea. I cannot see how we can justify a constable at a family funeral, especially at three in the afternoon. We cannot attend every funeral, can we? And this particular one is not very convenient from our point of view.'

'That's what I thought, Sergeant,' I said. 'It's right in the middle of the busiest time. I'll call Sir Giles and tell him we can't oblige on this occasion.'

'Who did you say?' he responded.

'Sir Giles Pifflington,' I answered. 'From Gelderslack House. You know it, Sergeant, it's just over the bridge on the Gelderslack to Whemmelby Road; that big stone house with the coat-of-arms on the gates.'

'You mean *the* Sir Giles Pifflington?'

'I don't follow,' I had to admit.

'Among his varied work, much of which is at national level, he is a member of the Home Office advisory committee on police finance, mutual aid agreements and crime prevention,' said Sergeant Craddock. 'A most important man by any standards. I thought you would know that!' he added pointedly.

'He did say he was a friend of the chief constable,' I bleated.

'I should say he is!' breathed Craddock in awe. 'Well, PC Rhea, this alters things somewhat. Look, I think you should attend.

Leave Ashfordly to me, I shall find someone to take your place in town – I might even do the task myself – so you go along to the funeral. What time did you say it was?'

'The cortège leaves the house at three,' I confirmed.

'And how long would you think it will continue?'

'Well, normally, the service is about three-quarters of an hour, then there's the interment, and the dispersal of cars from the church ... say an hour and a half at the outside. I need to be at the gates of Gelder-slack House in good time to make sure the cortège emerges safely on to the main road, so I should get there at twenty minutes to three or thereabouts,' I suggested.

'Very important, yes. Then when it's over, you can come straight down to Ashfordly to supervise the last of the show traffic as it goes away?'

'Yes, no problem, Sergeant.'

'Right, consider it done, and make sure you wear your best uniform. We want to impress Sir Giles with our smartness and efficiency, do we not?'

'Yes, Sergeant.'

I rang Sir Giles to assure him that I would present myself at the gates to his house well in advance of three o'clock tomorrow afternoon, and I would remain on duty until I felt it was prudent to leave.

'Thank you, Constable,' he said. 'I do appreciate this, but I don't think we shall detain you too long. It is not a large affair and I don't anticipate many mourners, but our exit can be dangerous at times. Now, before the interment, there will be a short service in the family chapel, that's in the grounds of the house, and, of course, that will conclude before we depart at three. At three, the procession will leave the grounds and head directly for the graveyard, and I expect we shall be there, at the graveyard, for a further twenty minutes at the most. That's all.'

'Oh, I see. Thank you for telling me. I'll be there around two forty.'

'Good man, and thank you.'

The fact that the service was in the family chapel and not the parish church would reduce my commitment considerably, but I felt I did not need to explain this to Sergeant Craddock. I would simply report to Gelderslack House tomorrow afternoon and cope with matters as they arose, and then head for Ashfordly as soon as it was over.

Having explained things to Mary, she said she would ensure my shirt was freshly ironed, and I would press my best uniform trousers. To present myself to a man who held such an eminent position in this country, I would ensure I was as smart as possible. I realized, of course, that the cream of local society would be attending. Perhaps the chief constable would be there too?

As I contemplated that duty, however, I did ponder, only slightly, about the fact I had heard nothing of this family death. Usually, when a member of an eminent local family dies, news of the event reaches most of us within a very short time and, of course, it often generates a paragraph or two in the local newspaper. On occasions of that kind, I was usually informed by the priest, vicar or undertaker, too. I liked to be kept informed of forthcoming funerals so that I could arrange to be present outside the church whenever possible, but in this case, the news had been sprung upon me. I'd heard nothing of the death and did wonder if, perhaps, the deceased was a family member from some distant place who had been brought home for burial? That happened from time to time, particularly with the county families. But, in reality, it did not matter to me who the deceased might be – it was a private matter and not my concern! All I had to do was guide the cortège from the house and on to the main road without causing an accident, and with the minimum of disruption. And then I had to do likewise as it turned off the main road to enter the graveyard. I was a simple task and I could foresee no complications.

After lunch on that Saturday, therefore, I left my house in a uniform so smart, and with boots so polished, that onlookers might have thought I was heading for a garden party at Buckingham Palace. I had washed and waxed my police van too, and it gleamed in the bright August sunshine as I motored across the purple moors towards Gelderslack. I had allowed plenty of time to park my van safely at a discreet distance from the house, and then walk to the entrance to Gelderslack House well in advance of the funeral procession.

Knowing the village very well indeed, I would use a short cut which would take me to the church. I could hurry through it once the cortège was clear of the gates of Gelderslack House and reach the entrance to the churchyard well ahead of the slow-moving cortège – thus it would be no trouble, manning both traffic points.

I arrived at Gelderslack House gates almost precisely at 2.40 p.m. and positioned myself so that I could peer along the drive to get an advance warning of the approach of the cortège from the house. Then I settled down to wait. I could see the bulk of the great house behind some trees, but there was very little activity around the gate. It took but a moment's reflection for me to realize that the mourners would all be safely inside before my arrival – they'd be attending the service in the family chapel. As I had never been inside the grounds, I had no idea of the exact location of the chapel, but as I studied the scene within the boundaries of the grounds I could not see any funeral cars, private cars or even the hearse. It made me realize that the grounds must be very extensive if such an influx of motor vehicles could be accommodated in such a way that all were completely concealed from the road. The lack of activity within the range of my vision probably meant that the chapel, with extensive parking space, was somewhere behind the main house.

And so, believing that everything was going smoothly, I settled down to await the arrival of the hearse. As I did so, I wondered how things were progressing with the show traffic in Ashfordly – I guessed it would be much more hectic than standing beside the impressive entrance to a grand country house in one of our more remote villages.

Three o'clock passed without any evidence of activity and then, at about five past, I heard the sound of an oncoming vehicle, but it was not the gentle purr one would expect from a well-maintained hearse. It sounded more like a tractor and almost the same instant I heard it, I saw it approaching from the direction of the mansion, having emerged from the buildings at the rear. It was a farmyard tractor and it was moving at a very slow pace with several people walking beside it, some at either side. There were two cars behind it and I wondered if this was some kind of advance party *en route* to the graveyard. I waited patiently for the procession to reach me, realizing that it would be sensible, due to its slow pace, to halt the main-road traffic in good time to allow it to exit on to the highway slowly but in complete safety.

As the tractor drew closer, I saw it was towing a trailer bearing a large oblong box made out of wood and painted black, and on top of the box was a straw hat with a band of flowers around it. Also on top, I could discern what appeared to be bridles and halters, while around the box, on the trailer, were bales of straw topped with more flowers. Marching beside the tractor and trailer were members of Sir Giles' family – I recognized his four teenage daughters, Sir Giles himself, his wife and some other children whom I did not know.

The following cars contained the more elderly members of the family – I noticed Sir Giles's mother in the rear seat of one car and another elderly lady in the other car – but there was no one else. This was no advance party – it was the actual funeral procession.

It was at that point I realized they were not burying a human being – they were burying a large animal of some sort, a horse by the look of the adornments on board the trailer. Then Sir Giles spotted me and shouted above the noise of the tractor.

'Jolly decent of you to turn out, Constable,' he boomed. 'We couldn't let poor old Neddy pass away without some sort of fond farewell.'

'Of course not,' I heard myself respond. 'So you are not going to the churchyard?'

'No, of course not; we're heading for our

own pets' graveyard, it's on the eastern edge of the estate. Down the lane a couple of hundred yards along the road ... follow us if you wish ... we may need you to halt traffic to let us turn off the road.'

'Yes, sir,' I said, thinking that Neddy was not the name one would give a horse. It was more of a donkey's name. And so, resplendent in my best uniform, I halted the oncoming main-road traffic to permit the cortège to gain the main road, turn right and head for the pets' graveyard at walking pace.

I followed, more out of curiosity than necessity, only to realize that I looked rather like a police escort to this curious procession because I did wave a few items of traffic past when the road was clear. At the point where the tractor needed to turn right into the lane leading to the graveyard, I hurried ahead, halted the main-road traffic and guided the agricultural hearse across its path and safely into the quiet lane, itself a private part of the estate. The foot mourners and two cars followed sedately.

The graveyard was about 400 yards along the grass-surfaced track, a plot of well-tended land within a wooded area, and as I walked behind the tractor and its retinue, I could see little wooden crosses and stone tombstones, but in the far corner, a massive hole had been excavated for this coffin. A mechanical digger stood by, waiting to fill in the hole once the interment was over, and so the tractor inched towards the grave then reversed into position whereupon the driver activated some hydraulics which raised the front of the trailer so that the big black box slid off the rear and into the hole, making good use of strategically placed planks of wood. It was a very well executed affair, I felt, and I could see two of the little girls weeping as the digger began to shovel in masses of wet brown earth.

As the family watched these final moments, Sir Giles came across to me.

'Neddy,' he said. 'Our faithful donkey. Been with us years. The girls were upset when he went to that great carrot field in the sky. Jemima says donkeys go to Heaven so we had a little service in the chapel ... all very sad stuff, Constable, but if you've a family you'll know how things are. We had to do something formal about it.'

'I understand perfectly,' I assured him. 'I remember one of my daughters burying her goldfish in the garden. She dug a grave, popped him in and said, "In the name of the

Father and of the Son and into the hole he goest". He had a good send off too, just like your Neddy.'

'We've generations of dogs, cats, ferrets, horses, calves and even a pet badger in here,' he said. 'Jolly good idea, pets' grave-yards. But I mustn't keep you. I do appreciate your attendance, it got us all safely here in a very seemly manner.

As I walked away, I cast a final glance at the family assembled around Neddy's grave; from a distance, it did look something like a conventional funeral with the flowers, the grave and its heap of waiting soil, the crosses and tombstones and the sad expressions on young faces, some with tears flowing down their cheeks. I wondered what kind of service they'd held in the family chapel, but it was no longer my concern. It took a few minutes for me to regain my parked Mini-van, and now I would head for Ashfordly, to deal with more mundane police matters like traffic control on a larger scale.

I decided, though, that it would be wise not to inform Sergeant Craddock that my valuable time had been spent directing three vehicles involved in the burial of a donkey. When I regained my police van, therefore, I booked on air with Ashfordly Control and it was Alf Ventress who asked, 'What's your location, Nick?' I thought he sounded rather flustered.

'Gelderslack,' I confirmed. 'Just leaving after funeral duties.'

'Can you get to Ashfordly as soon as possible? We've a bit of a crisis here.'

'Will co,' I acknowledged, adding, 'What sort of a crisis?'

'There has been an accident at the junction where Sergeant Craddock was on traffic duty. A cattle truck with fifty pigs on board collided with a car transporter carrying eight new Fords. The cattle truck veered into a building, that shop on the corner ... the doors burst open and all the pigs have escaped, Nick. I'm co-ordinating the search for them. Sergeant Craddock is sorting out the traffic in town and, of course, the first of the home-going show traffic will soon be leaving the ground...'

'Sounds like a busy time, Alf,' I said.

'You could say that,' he muttered. 'Just get yourself here, will you? Come to the office, I'll brief you on the details when you arrive.'

'Will co,' I smiled, wondering what sort of fun I'd have rounding up dozens of pigs. It might be an idea to go home first, to change into a more suitable uniform – unless, of course, I finished my day's duty by attending the funeral of some pigs. Maybe smart attire would be needed?

With the help of some of the farmers attending Ashfordly Show, we rounded up every one of those escaped pigs but I never did tell a somewhat harassed Sergeant Craddock that my absence had been spent attending the funeral of a donkey.

Attending what are, in the mind of a hardened inner-city police officer, unnecessary minor events, was very much part of the daily routine for a rural constable. One example occurred when I received a call from Mrs Henrietta Wytherstone of Shelvingby Hall. She and her husband, Harold, were leading lights in the local Conservative Party and they decided to host a money-raising event at her home. The Conservatives were in urgent need of funds and the event, to be held on the second Saturday of July, would comprise a rather superior garden party within the spacious grounds of their home. There would be a marquee should the weather be unpleasant and Henrietta had spoken to her friends in various ladies' luncheon clubs, the WI and elsewhere with a view of having a range of interesting stalls.

They would sell things like craftwork, home made wine, cakes and other produce, beside which would be a tombola, a raffle, music from Brantsford Brass Band, displays of local products and horsemanship, a wonderful buffet lunch with wine and champagne – at a cost – and many other attractions. Henry, a lover of classic cars, was arranging with his friends to bring their prize vehicles for display and their two sons, now in their twenties, had arranged for a mock battle to be staged between the Cavaliers and Roundheads. They had re-cruited some of their friends for that event. Overall there would be a fat entrance fee, the idea being to attract the wealthy, deter the riff-raff and raise lots of money for Conservative funds. As the couple had a wonderful collection of porcelain, furniture, artefacts from Africa, valuable original oil paintings and historic books, the ground floor rooms of the house would also be open for viewing – in some respects, it would be akin to a tour of a stately home, albeit on a smaller scale. Guides would be positioned in all the open rooms, both for security and to provide information about the items on display – I would discuss security matters with Mrs Wytherstone prior to the day. The whole shindig would begin at 11.30 a.m. with lunch at 1 p.m. as the highlight, and it was expected to conclude around 5.30 p.m., after a good time had been had by all.

Well in advance of the date, I received a call from Mrs Wytherstone asking if I could be present on the day, in uniform, to act as a general overseer of good behaviour with particular emphasis on car parking, entrance to the grounds, keeping out unwelcome visitors and so forth. My lunch would be provided free of charge and if I wished, I could take my family, again free of charge.

Strictly speaking, our attendance at private functions of this kind, held on private property, was something we could hardly regard as official police duty. In the case of major events, like race meetings, a charge was made for our services and the legal question of whether we were private individuals or police officers for the duration of such 'hire' was always open to question. In the case of smaller events, like the garden party at Shelvingby Hall, however, it was customary to attend in uniform. Our work on such occasions was considered good public relations rather than a necessary police duty. When I was conducting traffic on the road outside the Hall, however, I would be officially on duty – it was a public road and I would be doing traffic duty – but once inside the grounds, then it was questionable whether I was 'on duty' or attending in a private capacity. Apart from patrolling the grounds during the festivities, I would visit those rooms open to the public, just to show the uniform in the hope it might deter any potential thieves. For those who saw me in my uniform I was regarded as a policeman – they were unaware of the niceties of the legal aspects – and as such, my presence – with the knowledge and approval of my senior officers – was always considered an essential part of the proceedings.

Prior to the garden party, I visited Mrs Wytherstone on several occasions to determine precisely what was to happen within the grounds, to discuss security of valuables within the house and to satisfy my own need to know the precise extent of my responsibilities. I came away with the impression that she was a most capable administrator who seemed to run things at home while her husband concentrated upon his business which, I understood, was something to do with merchant banking.

On that Saturday in July, therefore, I reported my presence to Mrs Wytherstone, a very tall handsome woman with a beautiful face, blonde hair, impressive figure and wonderful clothes. In her middle fifties, she enjoyed the very best of health in a world where money was of no consequence, but I do know she helped many of the local charities without seeking any reward or appreciation. I found her very likeable and approachable. It was a hot and sunny day when I arrived at the house; I was pleased because fine weather made life so much easier and infinitely more enjoyable when working in the open air. Feeling very content, therefore, I went into the kitchen to find Mrs Wytherstone.

She was supervising her personal staff who were preparing their contribution to the lunch – and she provided me with a coffee and a bun, saying the Conservative ladies and WI members were in the marquee, busy finalizing their contribution to the meal. Her husband and sons, Jeremy and Oliver, were somewhere in the grounds, making sure the other features were all in place and that everything was functioning. Thanking Mrs Wytherstone for the coffee, I went off to perform the first of my roles – traffic duty.

This was on the road outside and we expected a regular flow in visitors between 11.30 and 12.30, with lunch due to start at one o'clock. My job was to usher the cars safely into the grounds, dividing them alternatively into left and right lanes from where a couple of attendants would guide them to separate ends of the parking field. The system of sending one to the left and one to right meant that neither attendant was inundated with a long queue; he felt he could cope with them coming at him if there was a short delay between each.

Once the cars were parked, the party-goers were directed towards a gate, standing open, beside which had been positioned a pair of ticket booths, one at either side. People paid their dues, or showed their pre-purchased tickets, and were then admitted to the festivities. It all seemed to be very well arranged. There were 'No Parking' signs along verges outside the house and Mrs Wytherstone had indicated I should expect several hundred cars, along with other vehicles like horse boxes and a coach carrying the brass band.

The Hall's main gate was highlighted by lots of posters with white lettering on a blue background, with some saying, 'Entrance' and others announcing 'Parking' with arrows showing the direction. I was extremely busy during that hour for the cars were pouring into the grounds, many with four people on board and from what I could discern, the parking arrangements were working very smoothly with people being admitted to the grounds with the minimum of delay. This turn-out proved it was indeed the social event of the summer so far as the people of this district were concerned. Hundreds were pouring in and I felt sure the whole day would be a massive success and that the Conservatives would benefit greatly – even if I, as a police officer, had to remain neutral (like members of the Royal Family) so far as party politics were concerned.

With surprising speed, the time approached ten minutes to one and the incoming traffic had dwindled almost to nothing as lunch-time approached. That was the signal for me to abandon my traffic point and head for the marquee, there to avail myself of the promised free lunch. Afterwards, I would patrol the house and grounds at my discretion, dealing with the inevitable range of queries and problems like lost children, lost purses, the way to the toilets and so forth, before returning to my traffic point in time to usher the flood of vehicles safely away from the house. As I was about to depart for my lunch, however, a sleek maroon Rover 2000 eased to a halt before me. The windows were slightly darkened so I could not see who was in the rear seat, but the driver was clad in a smart suit, white shirt and dark tie. Sitting beside him in the front passenger seat was another man in a dark suit. I was standing in the middle of the road, just outside the entrance, and so the man in the passenger seat lowered his window to speak to me.

'Is this Shelvingby Hall?' he asked.

'It is,' I replied, thinking this must be some VIP guest, although my immediate reaction was that if Mrs Wytherstone had anticipated or invited some person of note, then she would have warned me in advance. And she hadn't.

'Something's happening here?' was his next question, eyeing the 'Entrance' and 'Parking' signs on display.

'It's a garden party,' I responded. 'If you want to go in, just follow that road to the right–'

'A garden party?' he interrupted me, his eyebrows rising quizzically. 'For a particular purpose, is it?'

'Yes, for Conservative Party funds,' I said. 'Mr and Mrs Wytherstone are hosting the event, lunch is about to be served...'

At this, the man to whom I was speaking turned to the anonymous man in the rear seat and said, 'Well, sir, do we or don't we?'

'I must not be seen to show favour to any political party,' said the voice and when I bent lower to get a view of him, I saw it was a very youthful man whom I shall refer to as Prince X. 'I must not even hint that I may be supporting this event...'

At that moment, another car arrived, pipped its horn to show some slight annoyance at being delayed in this manner, so I waved it past, and directed it to take the right hand route. The driver sailed on, little realizing who had held up his rush to arrive for the start of lunch.

'Perhaps the constable could inform Jeremy Wytherstone that you are here?'

'I must admit I could do with what is known as a comfort break,' laughed the Prince.

'Is there a place not being used by the Conservatives?' asked the man whom I now realized was a personal detective. He'd be from Scotland Yard's Royal Protection Squad. 'A room in the house perhaps?

Somewhere His Royal Highness can go without being seen by anyone – other than the family, of course?'

'Just the kitchen, sir.' I decided I would address the detective as 'sir' – I knew he'd carry the rank of detective inspector at least, probably even superintendent. Besides, I realized my remarks were also being addressed to His Royal Highness.

'You know the way?' the detective asked.

'I do, sir, yes. I know the layout of the house. I've been around it, checking security for today's event.'

'Good,' said the Prince. 'Then perhaps you can lead us to the back entrance? And into the kitchen? And find one of the Wytherstones for me?'

'Yes, sir, yes of course.'

And with that, the rear door opened and I was invited to join the Prince on the rear seat as the unremarkable car entered the grounds. By now, I was sweating and very nervous, but the Prince was charming, asking me where I was stationed and whether I enjoyed my work. I told him it was always interesting, and always exciting, one aspect of which was that we never knew what was going to happen next. In directing the car, I avoided the routes to the parking area and guided the driver towards the rear of the Hall, not the most glamorous of areas with its array of dustbins and outbuildings. The rear door was at the top of a short flight of steps and so I left the vehicle and led the way. I thought the royal party would remain in the car until I had cleared the route ahead but they didn't; the chauffeur leapt out to open the rear door as the detective emerged from the other side and suddenly I was being followed into Shelvingby Hall by Prince X and his detective.

I led the way through the corridor towards the kitchen and, happily, the place was deserted. Everyone was now in the marquee for lunch, the helpers included, and so this part of the house was deserted. As we approached the kitchen, the detective asked, 'Loos?'

'On your right,' I said, indicating a door shown to me by Mrs Wytherstone during one of my visits.

Without a word, Prince X vanished inside as I waited with the detective.

'Detective Superintendent Stan Rackham, A1, Royal Protection,' he introduced himself.

'PC Nick Rhea,' I shook his hand. 'Village bobby at Aidensfield, sir, a few miles from here.'

'Sorry to spring this one on you, Nick, but he was at school with Jeremy Wytherstone,' he told me. 'He likes to pop in like this, on old friends he can trust. It helps break our journey; we're on our way from Scotland back to London.'

'I'd better find Mrs Wytherstone,' I said.

'Show us into the kitchen first,' he said. 'We'd all like to pay a call, the chauffeur included.'

'There's food galore,' I said.

'Now you're talking!' he grinned, and the Prince reappeared looking decidedly happier.

'Thanks,' he smiled.

'The kitchen is this way, sir,' I said, pointing and then leading them. When we entered, it looked as if a bomb had hit the place – there was food, plates, crockery, unwashed utensils, bottles of wine and more besides, littering every surface including the huge oblong table in the centre. But the place was deserted.

'I'll go and find Mrs Wytherstone,' I said.

'Not a word about who is here!' Superintendent Rackham. reminded me.

'Could you find Jeremy, too?' asked Prince X.

'Yes, sir,' I assured him and left the kitchen

to emerge through the front door on to the grand lawns of this mansion. There would be no trouble locating the family, everyone was crowded around the marquee; they had obtained their food from the tables inside and had then adjourned to the spacious lawns to enjoy an *al fresco* lunch. Among the crowd, it took me a while to identify Mrs Wytherstone but eventually I spotted her. I made my way through the densely packed crowd and hailed her, but she simply waved her hand and said, 'Well done, PC Rhea, we got them all in without any trouble, so get a plate and help yourself.'

'Er, I'd like a word,' I said. 'Alone, please.'

'Oh, can't it wait? I am hosting this event, as you can see, and I must meet as many guests as I can...'

'It can't wait,' I insisted. 'I must speak to you alone. Sorry,' I apologized to the knot of people to whom she had been chatting. 'And your son, Jeremy, if we can find him.'

Her faced blanched. 'Oh, dear, something's happened ... Jeremy was over there, with the Brownings ... look, there...'

'You go up to the house,' I spotted him chatting to a group of young women. 'Jeremy and I will catch you up, but I must have a word before you go in.'

I now had her undivided attention, but felt I should break the news to both her and her son at the same time. She was becoming very agitated and I knew they would have to devise a joint strategy to cope with their unexpected visitor and so I was pleased I had persuaded her to wait until I had summoned Jeremy.

I caught Jeremy, a cheerful young man with a loud laugh and a delightful sense of humour, and asked him to join his mother and I on the front steps. Mrs Wytherstone trotted across the lawn to join us; we were well away from the crowds who seemed to be ignoring us. If they did see us chatting, they would think it was some routine matter which required attention.

'What is it, PC Rhea?' She was growing angry now. 'I do hope this is something important, dragging me away from my guests.'

'Prince X is in your kitchen,' I said quietly. 'With his detective. He's on his way to London and popped in to see Jeremy.'

'I do hope this is not your idea of a joke, PC Rhea.'

'It's not. He's there,' I said firmly. 'And he can't join the festivities, he can't even let himself be seen here, as he can't be thought

171

to favour any political party.'

'Oh my goodness ... you are serious, aren't you? Oh, dear what can I do? Jeremy, what can I do?'

'Don't panic, Mother, he doesn't like a fuss. Let's go and see him, I'll introduce you and if I know His Royal Highness, he'll love a quick bite to eat at the kitchen table, then he'll be on his way within half an hour.'

'But the kitchen, it's in such a terrible mess...'

'He won't mind!'

'You'd better come in too, PC Rhea, for your lunch,' she said.

'No thanks,' I said. 'I can't intrude on this. I'll find myself something in the marquee.'

'The dining-room isn't being used yet, is it?' she asked Jeremy. 'The visitors will be going round the house after lunch ... maybe we could use that?'

'Stop panicking, Mother,' grinned Jeremy. 'At school, the prince liked nothing better than mucking in with ordinary people, doing ordinary things. Come along, I think we can find a clean plate and perhaps a mug with his mother's picture on it.'

'You will apologize to them down there, won't you, PC Rhea? For my absence?'

'I think the less is said, the better,' I

suggested. 'There are enough people enjoying that lunch for everyone to think you are still among the others, meeting and greeting them all. I don't think you'll be missed.'

'He's right. Come along Mother, and meet your Prince.'

As I approached the marquee intent on finding a plate and some food, Harold Wytherstone hailed me.

'Ah, PC Rhea, I saw you heading for the house with my wife and Jeremy. Not trouble, I hope?'

'No,' I said. 'Just a small domestic matter to be sorted out in the kitchen. I'm sure she will explain later.'

'The kitchen's her department, I have no wish to interfere. Well, come along, find yourself a plate and enjoy yourself. Get stuck in, you've earned it today.'

I did not see the departure of the royal car; it left the premises whilst I was inspecting some of the stalls and wondering whether, in uniform, I should tackle some of the contests.

Later, I was assured that no one, apart from the immediate family, knew that a member of the Royal Family had popped into Shelvingby Hall that afternoon – and had insisted on having only a light snack in the kitchen.

When I had completed my duties, however, I received a call from Sergeant Craddock. 'Did everything go smoothly at Shelvingby Hall?' he asked.

'No problems at all,' I assured him. 'It was planned to perfection. It went like clockwork – just like a royal visit in fact.'

Chapter 6

If much of my duty seemed to revolve around large country houses, then this was quite normal for my beat. There were lots of large country houses on my patch. The area was replete with wealthy people, members of the landed classes and aristocracy whose families had occupied these houses for generations. Many were estate owners with an income from rented properties and investments, but others were very hard-working people. A fine example of the latter was the Crabtree family who lived at Brockrigg Hall, a beautiful stone house just outside the remote hamlet of Lairsbeck.

Although this was a large country house, it was also a working farm even if Ben Crabtree did belong to that class of person known as a gentleman farmer. He had money, of that there was no doubt; he and his forebears had made their wealth through hard work and enterprise in rugged moorland conditions, so Ben did not struggle to survive like some hill farmers around him.

He did work hard, however, and employed several farmworkers to deal with his live-stock and agricultural crops, along with a groom to tend his horses. In addition, his wife, Laura, ran her own catering business. She provided fine foods for upmarket weddings, funerals and social events in the district and, in spite of having to work for a living, the couple mixed comfortably with the upper classes of the district. The Crab-tree family had owned the Hall since the day it was built and, through having to cope with hard times as well as easier ones, they had always worked for their living, making the splendid house pay its own way.

With portions dating to the sixteenth century, the magnificent house still stands on an elevated site behind a high grey stone wall. It is just across the bridge as one enters Lairsbeck from Ashfordly, but the house is shielded from the road by a copse of spectacular chestnut trees. Behind them, the ground rises slightly to the point where Brockrigg Hall is beautifully positioned with panoramic views to the south and west, and also taking in the windswept moors to the east. The entrance, on the northern part of the property, is from the road which passes through Lairsbeck, and the main gate is impressive to say the least. A couple of huge grey stone pillars form the gateway with a pair of ornate iron gates hanging between them. The gates are painted black with gold embellishments, and there is a family crest in the middle, the centrepiece of which is a badger with the familiar black-and-white striped face. The grey of its fur matches the colour of the gateposts and adjoining walls, but this is not the only badger to grace this entrance.

Standing firm on top of each gatepost is a massive stone badger. The pair stand on sturdy legs, each facing slightly inwards towards the other. Each has been carefully carved, far larger than lifesize, from a solid piece of local moorland granite of that unusual and distinctive grey colour. Even the texture of the fur has been captured in stone. The black-and-white faces of the animals have been crafted from appropriately coloured stone inserts, and even the tiny dark eyes have been fashioned from polished stones of the right colour. I was never sure whether the badgers were secured in some way atop their posts, or whether they remained there by weight alone.

From the view of a passerby, however,

they seemed to be standing without any security yet I doubted if even the most powerful gale would dislodge them.

There is little doubt the badgers are unique although no one is certain of their origins. The name of the sculptor is not known either, nor is the date of their creation. All that is known is that the badgers have been guarding that entrance as far back as the records can be traced. Brockrigg Hall is named after colonies of badgers which still live wild in the area, brock being an old English name for the badger. In the dialect of the North Riding of Yorkshire, a rigg is a ridge of high land, hence the name of the house. Inevitably, the two stone badgers have always attracted widespread attention, with tourists often stopping to take their photographs and, not surprisingly, they are the subject of an ancient legend which has appeared in almost every guide book to the district, along with photographs or drawings of the distinctive animals.

If one stands at that gate and looks away from the Hall, the ground slopes away through a woodland of deciduous trees and deep below, at the bottom of the slope, there is a small stream. Known in Yorkshire as a beck, it is this small waterway which gives Lairsbeck its name. The legend says that at midnight, when the harvest moon is shining across the rigg and when the chimes of Ashfordly parish church clock can be heard in the distance, the badgers descend from their perches, walk down the hill to the beck and drink their fill. Each of those conditions has to be present before the badgers undertake their journey – for example, the chimes of the clock can only be heard if there is no wind, or if the wind is blowing from the south-west.

The badgers return before the same clock strikes one by which time the moon has vanished behind that rigg of high moorland.

It is a wonderful old story and the tale is told of would-be badger-spotters waiting near the gates in order to catch sight of this occasional miracle but, of course, if people are watching, then the badgers do not move – even if the necessary conditions prevail. They remain in their fixed positions, moon or no moon, chimes or no chimes, just like blocks of ancient rock.

It was with knowledge of this legend that I was patrolling the lonely road into the dale of Lairsbeck early one fine September morning. I wanted a good start to the day because I was booked for a dayshift, which meant I had the evening free. For a village policeman, an evening free from duty was indeed to be treasured and I wanted to be sure I completed all my outstanding tasks before the end of my shift.

Lairsbeck is the name of the dale as well as the hamlet located there; there is but a handful of houses and farms, but I had to make the occasional trip into the dale to check stock registers and firearms certificates. On this occasion, as I always did, I glanced at the twin badgers as I passed the entrance to Brockrigg Hall but was surprised to see they had disappeared. I smiled to myself because the previous evening had witnessed the harvest moon –the full moon nearest to the autumnal equinox – and I wondered if the legend had come to fruition, or whether something more logical had occurred, like the badgers being removed for cleaning or maintenance. Thinking their removal for cleaning was most likely, I drove on, visited a couple of farms and then, around mid-morning started my return journey.

As I approached the badgerless pillars, I decided to visit Ben Crabtree – I could check his stock register in the normal way, and at the same time satisfy my curiosity. After easing my van to a halt outside his back door, I rang the bell and he responded; he was in the kitchen having a quick coffee and invited me to join him. I thanked him and his wife soon produced a steaming mug of delicious milky coffee and huge slab of fruit cake, then, without me asking, she went into his study and returned with his stock register. I let it rest on the table unopened until we had finished our social chatter, and then I said, 'Ben, those badgers on your gate...'

'Not you!' he laughed. 'You're the third this morning. First the postman, then the milk-tanker driver, and now you... I know all about it, Nick. It was harvest moon last night and the badgers are supposed to climb down and go for a drink ... and you're trying to tell me they've gone and haven't come back! Everybody's trying to catch me out with that yarn ... so all right, it's a good laugh, but I'm too old a hand to be caught like this. It happens every time there's a harvest moon in a fine night – folks try to tell me the badgers have gone down for their drink.'

'I'm serious,' I said. 'They have gone, Ben. I mean it.'

'I said you should have listened to the others!' snapped Laura. 'You've not even been to look, have you?'

'Look? Well, no, of course I haven't. I'm not falling for that. That's just what they want me to do, believe their tales and go looking. When you get your leg pulled like this time after time–'

'Ben, it's not a leg-pull.' I tried to appear very serious, but it was not easy in the circumstances. The affair was becoming very funny and it would be hard work making him believe me. 'Those badgers have gone. I thought you'd taken them down for cleaning, or to have something done to them like a repair, but they've gone. I'm serious. And if you haven't moved them, then someone else has – which means they've been stolen.'

'Nick, who in their right mind would steal a pair of heavyweight stone badgers like that? They're no good to anyone, and how would they get them down? They must weigh the thick end of half a ton each.'

'People do steal garden ornaments, Ben, large and very heavy garden ornaments. Things like stone lions, sundials, fountains, statues of Venus or whoever ... there's a big illicit trade in that kind of thing.'

He looked at me and said, 'All right, you've convinced me. Let's go for a look.'

Leaving our coffees unfinished, I took him down the drive in my van and together we went to view the topless pillars.

'Oh, God!' he groaned. 'You're right. How in the name of Beelzebub did they manage that? How could they move them and get them down from there?'

'The point is, Ben, they have got them down, or someone has, which means they've been stolen and we must try to find them. Were they here last night?'

'Yes, they were here at eleven,' he said with assurance. 'I'd been out to an NFU meeting and they were definitely on the pillars when I came back. I know, because there was a full moon and it reminded me of the legend.'

'They'd not gone for their drink by then?' I joked.

'No; I laughed to myself when I saw them, thinking they hadn't gone for that famous drink, so I do know they were there.'

'Well, they've gone now,' I said. 'We need to move fast. I can circulate a description through our own channels, but I think you need to do something that will reach a wider audience in the shortest possible time. The newspapers, Ben. The badgers are very well known, their pictures have appeared in all sorts of places, and if you could engineer that kind of publicity, with illustrations, it might just help us to trace them. I can't do that for you, I'm not supposed to feed information to the Press.'

'Right, leave that with me. I've good connections with the papers. And I have some photos of the badgers, in colour.'

'Right,' I said. 'Now, I need to do my formal bit; I have to compile a crime report.'

'You'd better come back to the house and I'll refill your coffee cup.'

With Ben and Laura in a state of mild shock and utter amazement at the audacity of the theft, I obtained the necessary details for my crime report, along with a photograph of the badgers. Their feet had not been cemented on to the surface of the pillars, their weight alone being sufficient to ensure they did not move even during the strongest gale. It was difficult placing a value on the statues but we settled for £1,000 the pair. He felt that, if the worst happened and they were not traced, then he was insured.

I would circulate the crime through police channels, but knew that the newspapers would provide a far better coverage than anything I could achieve. I left the couple to ponder the disappearance, wondering how anyone could have removed them without them realizing anything untoward was happening, but did prompt Ben to ring the local newspapers, television and radio stations with the minimum of delay. Then I left.

My first search was the area around the gates in case there were wheel marks or other evidence left by the thieves, but the tarmac surface revealed nothing. Then I walked down to the river-bank below the house in case some joker had decided to transport the badgers there, so they could get their legendary drink. But there was no sign of them and I got halfway home before I realized I'd forgotten to check and sign Ben's stock register. It could wait – there'd be another time for that. As I drove home-wards, my instincts told me that whoever had stolen these badgers had no idea of their widespread and unique fame, other-wise why steal them? They'd be instantly recognizable in any antique shop or second-hand dealer's emporium within miles of Ashfordly – and that gave me some reassur-ance. Their renown would suggest the thief or thieves might have difficulty disposing of them. Few handlers of stolen goods would touch something as instantly recognizable as these badgers, and if the thieves wanted to display them on their own premises, they'd be likewise identifiable. I began to think the thieves had blundered – but there again, a clever thief might already have spirited these things out of the country, or to some far-flung corner of Britain where these particular badgers were unknown.

I could take nothing for granted and for Ben and Laura's sake – and for the sake of local folklore – I hoped the press achieved the publicity necessary to locate these treasures. Before going home for lunch, I called at Ashfordly Police Station to notify Sergeant Craddock about the crime and he nearly blew a gasket when I revealed the value of the stolen goods.

'A thousand pounds, PC Rhea?' he gasped. 'Suppose they are not recovered? That means I shall have an undetected crime on my books with a figure of a thousand pounds beside it ... that is no good. I mean, what were they? Pieces of granite, lumps of stone ... you could have valued them at something reasonable, like a fiver each. How can such things be worth all that money?'

'It wouldn't surprise me if they were worth more,' I said, tongue in cheek. 'After all, they are very famous badgers, unique, I'd say.'

'Very well, what is done is done, and I am sure we shall be hearing from the Crabtrees' insurance company. Now, you need to circulate a description and we shall have to arrange visits to dealers, antique shops and so on, not just locally but over a very wide area.'

And so the routine procedures for dealing with this type of crime were put into action. Resting in the knowledge that everything that could be done was being done, I went home for lunch, then decided I would spend more time in Lairsbeck, just to see if anyone had noticed a vehicle or lifting gear in the vicinity during the night, or perhaps noticed anyone taking a rather intensive interest in those gate posts and their adornments.

In spite of the efforts I – and my colleagues – would make, I felt the Press would be our true salvation, although I had not mentioned that to Sergeant Craddock. Like so many experienced police officers, he was rather wary of the media and would have been horrified or even angry if I'd suggested any kind of Press involvement in detecting this crime. He saw such a crime as an indication that we were inefficient and he would worry that the Press might suggest that he tended to take such things rather personally but I knew he would not rest until we had recovered the badgers.

He did not rest. Even as I returned home at teatime to enjoy my evening off, he rang to ask if my enquiries had produced any worthwhile information and I had to admit I had not had the slightest success. I told him I had visited every house in Lairsbeck that afternoon to ask about suspicious vehicles or people in the vicinity of Brock-rigg Hall, but no one had seen or heard anything out of the ordinary. He responded by saying he had instructed the Ashfordly officers to saturate the town and outlying villages with enquiries and visits to all likely places of disposal, and to call upon all thieves known to take an interest in this kind of property. He reminded me to visit Claude Jeremiah Greengrass as soon as I could, even if I said Claude would never commit that type of crime.

'But I am sure he knows people who would!' returned Craddock.

Although I had promised to take Mary out

for a bar snack at a lovely inn some distance off my patch, my evening was dominated by thoughts of the stolen badgers. I found myself discussing it with Mary over our chicken-and-chips in a basket and she did add some useful comments, particularly as she was keen on gardening and had often seen similar artefacts on sale as garden furnishings. She did tell me of one or two outlets for that kind of thing and I jotted down the names in the back of my pocket diary. I returned home relaxed, but still wondering how and why the theft had been engineered.

At nine next morning, my telephone rang.

'PC Rhea?' snapped the distinctive Welsh voice of Sergeant Craddock. 'Have you seen the newspapers?'

'No, Sergeant,' I had to admit. 'Ours don't arrive until about half past nine or so.'

'Well, I suggest you get yourself down here as fast as you can and then explain to me how the theft of those badgers has come to be front-page news in the *Northern Echo*, page five news in the *Yorkshire Post* and even a note in the *Daily Mail* and *Daily Express*. Heaven knows where it's all going to end.'

'I didn't tell the Press, if that's what you are suggesting, Sergeant,' I felt I had to state my innocence at the outset.

'This kind of thing does no good for our image, PC Rhea. It makes us look inefficient and now we will have to face a barrage of questions about the crime. The Press will never be off our backs, asking if we've traced the property and if not, why not. And the public will become alarmed in case they become targets for similar crimes.'

'It might encourage them to take more care of their belongings,' I said.

'I don't think you understand the seriousness of this kind of uncontrolled publicity. It generates questions we need not have been troubled with, and it wouldn't surprise me if the Chief Constable himself has something to say about this.'

Upon his instructions, therefore, I drove down to Ashfordly Police Station where a copy of every daily paper was spread out across the enquiry office counter with items about the badgers being marked with large blue crosses.

'We're in the news, then?' smiled Alf Ventress as I went across to examine them. 'At least the public will know about the stolen badgers.'

'Ah, PC Rhea.' At the sound of my presence, Sergeant Craddock emerged from his office with an unhappy expression on his face. 'Have you seen this lot?'

'No, Sergeant, as I said, my papers haven't come yet.'

'You realize this could cause the thieves to smash up the badgers? To get rid of them where they will never be found? Dispose of the evidence before we can use it against them? This kind of thing does no good at all, most unhelpful to a professional police investigation.'

'It might help a member of the public to spot the badgers, Sergeant,' I countered. 'And it might stop anyone handling the badgers if they're offered by the thieves. There are times I think we should make use of this kind of publicity to help in the detection of crime.'

'Then you are in favour of this kind of thing?'

'I think there are times the Press and the police could work together for the greater good,' I smiled.

'And you have nothing to do with this splash?'

'No, Sergeant. I rather think Mr Crabtree will have engineered his own publicity, and there's nothing we can do to stop him doing that. After all, it is his valuable property we are talking about, and he wants it recovered if possible.'

'Might I suggest that, in future, if any such crimes occur, you advise the losers not to contact the Press in case it jeopardizes our investigations?'

'I'll bear that in mind, Sergeant,' I said.

In spite of the publicity, however, there were no reports of the stolen badgers being spotted by crime-fighting members of the public and our own enquiries over the next week or so failed to reveal any sightings of either the thieves, their vehicles and lifting equipment, or the badgers themselves. I visited Ben Crabtree several times during those days – and remembered to sign his stock register – but his own efforts had not produced any positive results. No one had called him to offer any kind of useful information whatever. In short, the badgers had disappeared into the night.

A further week or so passed without any hint of their whereabouts and our own investigation was gradually scaled down. We had exhausted all our usual avenues of enquiry without producing any useful information and even though the Press temporarily revived the story, complete with illustrations, in an attempt to jog the collective memory of the public, there was no response. I must admit I thought the badgers had disappeared for ever.

Then, one Sunday afternoon about three weeks after the theft, when I was in the office at Ashfordly Police Station, I received a telephone call.

'Is that Ashfordly police?' asked a Yorkshireman's voice.

'It is, PC Rhea speaking,' I confirmed.

'Aye, well, them badgers that went missing. Them stone ones, you know.'

'Yes?' My ears pricked up at his opening gambit.

'Well, I've found 'em.'

'You have? Where?'

'Under yon bridge at t'bottom of Oak Lea Bank, on t'beck side. With their noses in t'watter.'

'Are you sure?' I was slightly put off by the reference to them having their noses in the water. Was this some kind of on-going joke?

'Aye, 'course I'm sure. It's them what was in t'papers. Two of 'em. Stone.'

'Right, well, I'll come and have a look. Under Oak Lea Bank Bridge, you say?'

'Aye, that's it.'

'So who are you?' I needed his name for my eventual report, particularly if this turned out to be a genuine sighting.

'Nay, lad, I don't want my name splashing all over t'papers. I took a day off work to do a bit o' fishing, being a Sunday, and told the boss I had 'flu, so I'd better keep my head down ... anyroad, there they are. It's up to you lot now. God knows how they got there.'

'Thanks,' I managed to say before the phone went dead; the pips that sounded just before he replaced the handset told me he'd been ringing from a kiosk rather than a private telephone.

Wondering if this was some kind of practical joke, I decided not to mention it to Sergeant Craddock, or anyone else, until I had satisfied myself that these were indeed the missing badgers. Upon completing my business in the police station, I drove across to Oak Lea Bank, a twisting hill between Crampton and Brantsford. There is a small carpark at the summit where people tend to assemble during the summer months, either for picnics or simply to enjoy the view from the hilltop, but flowing through the dale, about 200 yards from the base of the hill, is the gentle River Cram. Where the river passes beneath the main road, a short distance from the foot of Oak Lea Bank, there is a stone bridge. The riverside at this point is a popular venue for fishermen and access to the water can be gained by going through a farm gate, across the corner of a field adjoining the road and then down to the water's edge. I knew it well – the area was, and still is, popular with visitors and ramblers as well as fishermen, for there is a riverside walk which begins at this point. It is possible to reach the water's edge by vehicle too, for in bygone times, a farm track crossed the river via a ford – that track still exists alongside the bridge and surfaced road. I arrived within twenty minutes or so, parked on the verge near the bridge, and walked along the track to the water's edge. As I did so, I sought evidence of vehicle tyre marks but there were no fresh marks and those which did exist were too weathered to be of any evidential value.

As I approached the water's edge close to the stonework of the bridge, I saw that the water was quite low and it had exposed a narrow shoreline of muddy sand, but when I looked under the arch, there were the two stone badgers. Each had been positioned with its nose over the water giving the impression of having a drink, although their feet were firmly planted in the sand at the edge. Their legs had sunk into the sand to a depth of some two or three inches but as I examined each one, I could see no damage. I tried to move them but it was impossible, they would not budge the tiniest of fractions. The suction generated by the mud, plus their enormous weight, meant some kind of lifting gear would be needed to recover them, to be hoped without damage. But how on earth had they been brought here?

I looked around for any sign of the anonymous caller but there was no one beside the river and although the sand was riddled with footprints, nothing was identifiable. It would be futile trying to trace both the caller and those who had placed the badgers here – although I would ask around the area to see if anyone had noticed any odd activity at the bridge in recent weeks.

Delighted at this development, I radioed Sergeant Craddock from my van. He had returned to the office by this time and responded with, 'Ashfordly Control.'

'Delta Alpha Two-Seven, Sergeant,' I gave the formal call sign of my van. 'Location, Oak Lea Bank Bridge near Crampton.'

'Receiving, go ahead,' he invited.

'The stolen badgers, Sergeant,' I said. 'I've

found them, both intact. They are under the bridge at this location.'

'What are they doing there?' he asked with some excitement in his voice.

'Having a drink of water!' I laughed.

'This is not a joke is it, PC Rhea?' He suddenly sounded serious.

'No, Sergeant, they are both safe and sound with no apparent damage, and they are standing on the mud at the edge of the River Cram.'

'Well, we shall need them positively identified by Mr Crabtree and we shall have to arrange their recovery and possible return to their owner. Do you think we need to retain them for evidence in any likely prosecution?'

'I doubt it, Sergeant; besides where on earth can we store two thirsty badgers who keep going walkies to look for drinking water?'

'We're not going to hear the last of this one, are we PC Rhea, thanks to all that Press coverage? And it will start all over again now, will it not?'

'It's all part of life's rich pageant,' was all I could think of saying.

'So how did you find them?' was his next question.

'An anonymous telephone call,' I told him. 'The finder was a fisherman, taking illicit time off work; he'd read about them in the papers, Sergeant, and when he saw them here, he rang Ashfordly police from a kiosk. I happened to take the call.'

'Well, I am surprised he doesn't want his name known; you'd think he would want a little of the reflected glory that will flow from discovering these items, but all's well that ends well. All right, wait there, I'll join you shortly – and I will ring Mr Crabtree with the good news. I will hope to fetch him with me to identify his property.'

The Crabtrees were delighted with the news and Ben said he would arrange collection of his badgers. He had friends with the necessary lifting gear, and said he could recruit a band of sturdy fellows who could manhandle the weighty objects if and when it became necessary. The Press had a wonderful time with the news, making much of the fact that the two badgers had taken to wandering in search of their drinks, but the thieves were never traced, nor did we discover how they had removed their trophies from the gate pillars. Whether the badgers had been taken direct to Oak Lea Bank Bridge as some kind of joke, whether they were intended to be sold by the thieves, and whether the Press coverage had prompted them to get rid of these hot items of stolen property, we never knew.

Ben did consider having replicas made for display on the gate posts, and keeping the genuine articles somewhat safer within the house or grounds, but on reflection, he felt that was not necessary. With heavy lifting gear, therefore, he replaced them in their former positions, but this time he lodged each foot in concrete.

'I reckon that will stop any thief removing them!' he said with pride.

'Won't that stop them going down for a drink at the river?' I laughed.

'That's the whole idea,' he grinned.

But in spite of that, the legend continues. So, if you happen to be passing Brockrigg Hall at midnight when the harvest moon is glowing, and you can hear the striking of Ashfordly church clock, you might just see two badgers heading towards the river for a drink of water. If you do, ring Ashfordly Police Station.

Another bridge featured in a series of crimes on my patch. It was the railway bridge which spanned the road between Thackerston and Ploatby, not far from Ploatby junction. Like so many railway bridges in this locality, it was a handsome structure comprising large blocks of stone all carefully trimmed and shaped. There was a large central arch under which the road passed, but at each side there was a smaller archway. These two additional arches rested in fields at either side of the road and served no other purpose than to be decorative. I suppose, when the bridge was built, those superfluous arches were a means of saving large amounts of stone during the original construction.

Because those two minor arches each spanned nothing more than a very small patch of field, however, they served as shelters for cattle, horses and sheep during inclement weather, and some farmers used them for storage. I've seen fodder kept in such places, and implements of various kinds could be accommodated beneath these useful shelters; campers also make use of them as sites for tents or campfires, while ramblers often rest there during their hikes if the weather is either very hot or very stormy. In fact, a footpath, now little used, ran through one of the arches of the Ploatby junction bridge. The path extended from

Thackerston to Ploatby and while it had once been in regular use – before the days of motor cars – it was now the preserve of a few ramblers and naturalists.

It was with this background that I received the complaint of a crime from Tom Featherstone. Perhaps the word 'complaint' is too strong in this case because Tom did not really expect an investigation into the matter he discussed with me.

Rather, he 'mentioned' it so that I could keep my eyes open for the culprit. The snag was that once a crime was 'mentioned' to a police officer, he or she was duty bound to investigate the matter if it proved to be a crime, and this entailed making a written record of the incident, followed by the necessary enquiries. Sometimes, this kind of formality was difficult for rural folk to understand – quite often, the crime in question was a very minor but troublesome affair and so they preferred to 'mention' such incidents, rather than make very formal and official complaints. Having 'mentioned' it, the last thing they expected was an almighty fuss with lots of paperwork and continuing enquiries; all they hoped for was that the constable would keep his eyes open and, if possible, deal with the perpetrator.

Tom Featherstone was the victim of a series of such very minor but very puzzling crimes. Tom was the local roadman. He was called a 'lengthman' and was responsible for the care of the highways and byways around Thackerston and Ploatby. He made sure the drains were clear, reported to the authorities if cracks or holes appeared in the surfaces, tidied up litter, trimmed verges and hedges, cleared snow, spread grit on icy patches and did a host of other tasks which kept the roads in good condition all the year round. His work was most useful and his efforts were appreciated by the local drivers and road users.

When I first encountered Tom, shortly after my arrival at Aidensfield, he was in his late fifties, a dour Yorkshireman of few words who lived in a cottage at Thackerston. He was married to Jennie, but there were no children, and his horizons had not spread beyond the tiny patch of Yorkshire in which he lived and worked.

Rather short in stature and somewhat plump in appearance, with a few days growth of whiskers permanently upon his round face, Tom always wore a black beret, a grubby old raincoat, black hobnailed boots and corduroy trousers. His trousers were bound below the knee with a length of hairy string. Someone said he always had string tied around his legs to prevent rats and mice or even stoats and weasels running up his trousers, should he disturb them during his road-tending or drain-clearing operations.

His mode of transport at work was an old pedal cycle, black in colour, which he maintained in prime condition – it was always clean, the chrome was polished and the chain well oiled. Tom's hobby was gardening; he grew masses of flowers, fruit and vegetables which he would sell for a few pence to anyone who called, while Jennie worked part-time in Thackerston Lodge as a cleaner. They were a lovely couple, kind-hearted and simple in outlook, while being undemanding of society; everyone liked them and if I saw Tom on his patrols, I would often stop for a chat. It was such a chat that produced his 'mention' of the crimes to which he was the victim.

'Now then Tom.' It was around half-past nine one Monday morning when I spotted him sweeping autumn leaves from the vicinity of a roadside drain. I eased my van into a convenient gateway and climbed out for one of my regular chats.

'Now then, Mr Rhea,' he nodded. 'Not a bad day for the time of year.'

We chatted about the weather, always a good opener for a rustic conversation and a topic of importance to country people, and then I asked if Tom had seen anything interesting or suspicious during his lonely patrols.

People like Tom, out and about during the day, did notice things which were out of the ordinary – strangers examining or visiting houses, cars being driven erratically or parked in odd places, smoke rising from supposedly empty premises, men knocking on doors of pensioners' houses and a host of other minor things. Tom was like an extra pair of eyes and ears for the police, and thus he helped in protecting our society. But on this occasion, he had his own mystery to relate.

'While you're here, Mr Rhea,' he said, 'mebbe I could mention summat?'

'Sure, Tom. What is it?'

'Well, mebbe it's nowt, but seeing you're here, I thought you ought to know.'

'OK, fire away.'

'You know I leave my bait bag under yon bridge, that 'un near t'junction?'

'Er, no, I had no idea,' I had to admit.

'Oh, aye, done it for years, I have. Yon bridge is right in t'middle of my roads, I've five roads to care for, you see, and there's an iron hook on t'wall under yon bridge, where I hang my bait bag. I can get there, no matter where I am, in less than five minutes on my bike, so I can have my dinner there, and my ten o'clocks and tea. It doesn't matter which road I'm seeing to, I can get back for my bait – and if it's wet, yon archway shelters me and if it's hot, I can get out of t'sun for a bit. And it's private; you don't get motorists gawping when you're sitting on t'verge having summat to eat. A lot of 'em think you're skiving. And bosses. They seem to think we all take too much time off for snacks. It's all very private, that bridge. That's why I allus go there for my breaks, but I do play fair, I allus knock my travelling time off.'

'It sounds very useful,' I agreed.

'Aye, very,' he nodded. 'I've allus said how special yon bridge is for me.'

I knew, of course, that his reference to bait was nothing to do with fishing, for many working men took a bait bag to work. It was usually a haversack or knapsack, and bait was a local term for a packed meal. Each working day, therefore, Tom's wife would pack his bag with bait which comprised enough food for his ten o'clock snack, his lunch or dinner as he called it, and something for an afternoon tea break. There'd be a vacuum flask, too, containing hot tea, enough for all three daily breaks, and little treats like an apple, orange or bar of chocolate.

'So you don't leave your bike under the arch, with your bait bag?'

'No, I need that for getting about on. From yon bridge to whatever pitch I'm working on. That's what I do, every day, when I start work.'

'Right, go on, Tom. Tell me your tale.'

'Well, last week, Monday it was, I went for my bait at ten o'clock, for my ten o'clocks, like I allus do, and there was nowt there. My bag was empty, well, not quite empty. My flask was there, full o' tea, but all the grub had gone.'

'Your sandwiches you mean?'

'Aye, two rounds of ham sandwiches, a scone, three slices of fruit cake, half a dozen chocolate biscuits, and an apple. All gone. Ten o'clocks, dinner and tea break, all vanished. Not a crumb left.'

'Maybe Jennie had forgotten to pack it, or perhaps you'd forgotten to take it with you when you left for work?' I thought this was the most logical explanation.

'I must admit that's what I thought at first, Mr Rhea. I thought she'd forgotten, but when I got home she swore she'd packed me up. She's very regular like that, very reliable, she allus packs my bait bag and hangs it over my bike crossbar ready for when I set off. I knew it was packed, because you can tell, the weight, you know. I didn't take an empty bait bag with me, I know that.'

'So you'd have a day without anything to eat?'

'Aye, there's no time to go home when you've a lot to get done and only half an hour dinner break and a few minutes for ten o'clocks, so I made do with my flask. I found a few brambles on t'hedges, though, and there's an apple tree growing wild on Thackerston Lane.'

'So you didn't starve?'

'Nay, I got an apple or two, but I must say it's a funny going-on, Mr Rhea.'

'You could have gone home, couldn't you? It's only a few minutes on your bike? To get extra food?'

'Nay, Mr Rhea, they'd think I was dodging work, skiving off. No, I dossn't go home in t'middle of a working day.'

'I don't think your bosses would have minded under the circumstances. Anyway, your bait: could an animal have taken it?' I knew that grey squirrels could perform all manner of thieving antics, but I doubted if they would or could get into a haversack of sandwiches to remove everything.

'Nay, it's got one of them brass fasteners on, a squirrel would never undo that, Mr Rhea. Anyroad, I thought I'd best mention it.'

'You did right,' I assured him.

'I thought there's a chance you might know what happened. You see, it happened all that week.'

'You mean you lost your bait every day?'

'Aye, every day last week,' he nodded fiercely.

'It's certainly not squirrels then.'

'Nay, Mr Rhea, not squirrels,' and he gazed intently at me as if expecting me to provide an instant solution to the mystery.

'So what else could be taking your bait?'

'Nay, now if I knew that I wouldn't be standing here talking to you, would I, Mr Rhea?'

'Well,' I said, after a moment of pondering, 'if someone is stealing your food, then we shall have to register it as a crime and launch an investigation. Do you think someone is stealing it?'

'Well, it's certainly a rum going-on but I'm not one for making a fuss about things, but I just thought you should know, so you could keep your eyes open. I thought I'd best mention it, seeing you're out and about and wanting to know about such things. You keep asking me if I've seen owt happening, so I knew you'd want to know about such goings-on.'

'You never take your bait bag with you then? When you go off to work?'

'No, I allus go under the bridge for breaks, Mr Rhea, so I leave my bag there. That's what I do and that's what I've allus done,' he said with an air of finality.

'So your bag is there now?' I asked.

'Aye, it is,' he said, looking at me once more as if I was going to perform a miracle of some kind.

'So the food might have gone again? This morning?' I put to him.

'Well, I haven't checked, Mr Rhea,' he said. 'It's not ten o'clocks time, you see.'

'But you left your bag there as usual, hanging on that hook under the bridge?'

'Aye, like I said, I allus do that. I never fail to go under the bridge for my bait times.

Very special place, is that bridge.'

'And you've never stayed behind to see if you could discover who or what was taking your food? I mean, you could have hidden somewhere, on the bridge itself, or behind a hedge or something, to try and catch the culprit.'

'No, I can't do that, Mr Rhea, I've got to get on to my pitch on time, otherwise they might discipline me.'

'They?'

'The council, my bosses, Highways. You never know when they're going to turn up and do a check, you see. Very keen on timekeeping, they are.'

'Well, I think we should go there now to check your bag,' I said.

'It's not my bait time yet, Mr Rhea. Ten o'clock is my time. From here, it'll take two minutes there, and two minutes back, that's four minutes. My ten o'clocks is ten minutes long, so I have six minutes' break time allowing time for travelling, and I go under the bridge for it.'

'It's nearly quarter to ten,' I checked my own watch. 'Look, hop into my van, I'll run you down to the bridge. If "they" grumble, I can always say you are helping me investigate a crime.'

'Well, if you're sure it will be all right, Mr Rhea. I don't want to get into bother for being absent from my pitch.'

'What about your bike?' I said. 'I don't want it stolen while we're away!'

'It's behind that hedge, Mr Rhea, well out of sight.'

And so, with some misgivings about the likely arrival of some boss or other, Tom joined me in the Mini-van and we drove the short distance to the railway arch. I parked on the verge and he led me through a farm gate and into the field through which the footpath ran, turning left along the back of the hedgerow. The railway bridge was a few yards ahead and even as we approached, I could see his khaki bait bag hanging from a stout metal hook on the wall of the bridge. It was well hidden from the road and not within reach of animals on the ground. I wondered whether the presence of the footpath bothered Tom – apparently, it didn't. I think he wanted to hide from 'them' – i.e., his bosses, not the general public on rambles and hikes. The area beneath the bridge comprised chiefly dried earth with no sign of footprints, although there were patches of thin grass, and the route of the path was clearly defined. It ran along the side of the hedge beyond the bridge and vanished around a distant corner, linking Thackerston with Ploatby.

'Well, there it is, Tom,' I said. 'Your bag's still there. Let's open it and see if we've had another crime.'

Even before looking inside, he said, 'They've been again, Mr Rhea look, the catch is undone, you can see it from here.'

And so it was. He lifted the flap, however, and a look of disappointment showed as he realized his precious food had vanished. The vacuum flask was there and it was intact, but every scrap of food had disappeared.

'Tom,' I said. 'I know this archway is very special to you, but I do think it would be wise not to leave your full satchel here tomorrow. You never know who's passing along this path. Take it with you, I'm sure you could find somewhere quiet for your breaks.'

'Aye, I might have to do that,' he said with a sigh of resignation.

'Look, I can run you home to get a refill, enough for today. We can go now.'

'Nay, Mr Rhea, you've done enough. I've been off my pitch long enough...'

I looked at my watch.

'Tom, it's your break time very soon. I can

get you home, find some food and have you back on your pitch before your break time is up. That's allowed, isn't it? By your bosses?'

'Aye, right, Mr Rhea, but you must admit it's a very rum going-on.'

'It is a rum going-on, Tom, but we can put an end to it simply by not leaving temptation in the way of the thieves.'

'I did right to mention it though, didn't I?'

'You did,' I assured him. 'Though I don't think it is the sort of thing that I can record as a crime. But I will try to find out who's been taking your food.'

I knew that if I recorded this as a crime, Sergeant Craddock would claim Tom's wife had forgotten to pack his meal, or that Tom had eaten it and forgotten, or that animals had raided the unattended bait bag. There was no way I could see Sergeant Craddock allowing this to be 'crimed', as we termed it.

'If I hadn't had to get on to my pitch on time, I could have sat and watched and mebbe nabbed the blighters, but there again, if I had sat and watched, they'd have seen me and wouldn't have done it,' he reasoned.

'They?' I didn't think he was talking about his bosses this time.

'Well, whoever's done it, Mr Rhea. It's

funny, though, vanishing at this time of day. Very early, not as if it's dinner time.'

'What time do you leave your bag here?' I asked.

'Twenty-past seven on a morning,' he said. 'I have to be on my pitch by half-past, you see.'

'So it could be someone who's using that footpath on a morning, every morning? A regular user?' I added for good measure. 'Not a rambler, it's happening during the week, too, not at weekends. And it's not an animal, Tom, I'm sure of that. As you say, it would never get that brass fastener undone. So we've someone who's using that path under the bridge every weekday. Any ideas?'

'Nay, Mr Rhea, as I said, I'm away before half-seven, so I never see anyone and by the time I get back at ten, the stuff's gone.'

'Well, that pins it down to a certain time of the day,' I said. 'Come along, Tom, off we go to your house, we'll get you stocked up for today. Now, tomorrow, you must take your bait bag with you, keep it with you. Once you've broken this routine, you might be able to return ... and you could always bike back to the arch anyway, to eat your meal, but keep your bag with your bike, in other words.'

'Well that's all right, unless it's pouring down or it's hot sunshine,' he countered. 'There's times my bag gets full of rainwater if it's outside and if it's hot, my sandwiches go all hard and dry, so that's another reason why I use the arch. All this carry-on means changing my routine.'

'Fair enough. I know it will be difficult, changing the habits of a lifetime, but let's remove temptation from the thief or thieves, just for the moment. That's the first thing to do. Remove the temptation.'

'Well, right, I'll give it a try,' he agreed.

And so, having failed to find footprints or other clues to the perpetrators, I took the bag off the hook, handed it to Tom and said, 'Right, let's get this refilled before your ten o'clock break is over!'

At Tom's house, Jennie grumbled and said she'd tried to persuade him to keep his bait bag with his bike at all times, but he just reiterated his wisdom about leaving it out in the rain or baking sunshine, and I could see she would never change his routine. He had his own way of doing things, and I felt I had done quite well to persuade him to retain his bag for a while. She produced enough food for that day, and, in fact, he and I sat down in his kitchen, where he enjoyed his ten o'clock.

I had a nice break with the couple and by the time we departed for his pitch, he was sure he would not lose any more of his precious bait. He said he would continue to eat under his 'special' bridge, beyond the gaze of 'them' but for a while, would not leave his bag unattended beneath the arches.

Although I puzzled about the loss of his sandwiches, I must admit it was not at the forefront of my mind during the following days, but around nine one morning I was driving beneath that railway bridge and decided to have another look at the scene of Tom's crime. My chief reason was to see if he had reverted to his old habit of hanging his bait bag on the wall, but was pleased to see it was not there. And then, in mud which had been softened by a gentle fall of rain during the previous night, I saw two sets of tiny footprints. They led from the Ploatby direction towards Thackerston – and their size told me they had been made by small children, but there was none from any accompanying adult. Schoolchildren! Very small ones too, judging by the size of their shoes. Helping themselves to Tom's sandwiches?

I knew the school bus left Thackerston around eight fifteen each morning and, in those days (the late 1960s), children walked considerable distances either directly to school, or to catch a bus. Ploatby was a very small village, with less than a hundred residents and few of them had children of primary school age. It would be a comparatively simple matter to trace the children who used this path. Before school turned out, I would make discreet enquiries in Ploatby to establish which children used that path, and then, when the children were at home, I would pay a visit to the household.

It took but a few minutes of discreet enquiries in Ploatby to discover that the Bruntons, who lived in Hillside Cottage, had two children – twins aged seven, a boy and a girl called Michael and Janet. I retreated from the village with that piece of information, patrolled the rest of my patch during the day and then, at four-thirty, decided to return to quiz these two prime suspects.

Hillside Cottage stood behind Home Farm, along a rising track from the main road through this tiny community, and it looked very neat and well kept. At my knock, a dark-haired young woman responded; she had a baby in her arms, and then two faces peered at me from behind her skirts. Twins, as alike as the proverbial two peas in a pod, a boy and a girl.

'Oh!' she cried when she saw my uniform. 'Oh, dear, Roy's all right, is he?'

'Roy?' I asked, momentarily baffled.

'My husband, he's in hospital, when I saw you I thought...'

'Oh, I'm sorry,' I said. 'No, I've not come with any news from the hospital.'

'Daddy fell off his motor bike,' chipped in the little girl. 'He's hurt his head and legs and things, and so he has to stay in hospital.'

'So how can I help?' she asked, as the infant squirmed in her arms.

'It's not easy,' I began. 'I'm PC Rhea from Aidensfield. Are you Mrs Brunton?'

'Yes, you'd better come in,' she invited. 'It's chaotic in here without Roy to lend a hand ... excuse the mess. Was it Roy you wanted?'

'Er, no.' I now felt as if I was intruding upon a family in distress and knew that the reason for my presence was trivial by comparison.

'Oh, well, you must be here for a reason,' she said. 'You can't leave me worrying about it. You can't go without telling me why you're here!'

She turned and walked into the house, so I followed as the twins regarded me with quizzical looks. She took me into the living-room, the floor of which was littered with toys, but which was otherwise clean and pleasant.

'So?' she almost demanded.

'Your children, the twins, walk to Thackerston each morning? To catch the school bus?' I began.

'Yes?' and I could see the concern in her face now. 'There's nothing wrong in that, is there? They're safe enough! It's only twenty minutes, in fields all the way, well off the road. Why? What's happened? Have they done something wrong? Anyway, they were on half term last week.'

'A man, Tom Featherstone, the lengthman at Thackerston, well, he leaves his bag of sandwiches under the railway bridge while he goes about his work.'

'And?'

'Someone has been helping themselves to them,' I smiled. 'A nice daily round of fresh sandwiches, cake, fruit...'

'Oh my God...' she blushed. 'Oh dear, this is dreadful ... they said somebody was leaving food out for them ... in a bag... Michael? Janet? What have you been doing? Those sandwiches under the bridge, they're not for you!'

'Yes they are. They are put there every day for us, Mummy, in a bag, and there is a drink too, but it's too heavy to carry so we just take the sandwiches and cakes and things.'

She plonked the baby on the settee and then, without inviting me to sit down, said, 'Roy's self-employed and when he's been off work for a while, there's no money coming in. It's been three weeks now and I had no money to give them for school dinners. I told them to help themselves from the pantry because I'm busy with the baby each morning. They have to learn to do things for themselves; they're old enough now. I did say that God would provide. We don't want free dinners, Roy would never ask for that, and I sent a note to the teacher saying we'd get back to normal when Roy returns to work. Thankfully, it was half term last week but they're back at school now.'

'We didn't have school dinners,' smiled Michael. 'They're not very nice and so we took our own.'

'But there was no bag for you this morning?' I put to them.

'No, not today, they must think it is still half-term. Maybe there will be a bag tomorrow?'

'I don't think so,' I said, although wondering if Tom had reverted to his old habits.

'Oh dear, I don't know that to say...' Mrs Brunton said.

'Don't worry about it. I'll have words with Mr Featherstone to tell him what has happened,' I said. 'But in any case, the children can't be prosecuted, they're too young and they did honestly think the food was for them.'

'That's me saying God will provide.'

'I'm sure you can get help if Roy is not working,' I said.

'It all takes time, with forms to fill in and so on, and he's a proud man, Mr Rhea, he doesn't like charity being offered. He's a painter and decorator; he works for himself and won't ask for help from anybody, the state or otherwise. He likes to do everything himself.'

'You can be proud of him,' I told her. 'Now. Michael and Janet, remember there'll be no food tomorrow, Mr Featherstone will not leave his bag under the bridge any more.

'You'll have to take something from home,

like I told you,' their mother said. 'There's plenty of stuff in the pantry and if I'm busy with Adam, you can pack your own dinner. And if there is a bag hanging under the bridge, leave it alone!'

As I left the household. I felt sorry for Mrs Brunton and her problems, then drove across to Thackerton to explain things to Tom and Jennie Featherstone. I went to the house, knowing that Tom finished work each day at half-past four. I was admitted with a smile and Jennie said the kettle was on. It was almost Tom's tea-time and so I joined them. I told them about the twins finding the bag and, thinking it was some kind of manna from heaven, had helped themselves.

I explained about Mrs Brunton's dilemma and her hectic, hand-to-mouth lifestyle while Roy was in hospital and not earning, then Jennie Featherstone said, 'Tom, I think you should go and see that poor young woman. Tell her you will place a bag under the bridge every morning while her husband is off work. I will make sure it contains enough food for those children. We have no family; we can afford to care for others less fortunate than ourselves. And make sure that Roy never knows about it...'

And so Tom did. Each schoolday morning, there was a distinctive green-coloured bag of food on another hook under that railway bridge. Tom's bag was there, too, and he continued to enjoy his bait under the railway bridge.

'Those twins come and see us now,' he said to me much later. 'We've never had grandchildren, Mr Rhea, but it feels as if we have now. I allus said that bridge was special sort of place.'

Chapter 7

I was in Aidensfield post office one Tuesday morning, off duty and in civilian clothes, and was trying to select a birthday card from the modest display. As I studied the range on offer, a tall, smartly dressed man in his late forties hurried in and began to examine the selection of magazines and newspapers on the rack next to me. As we tried to concentrate on our efforts, Claude Jeremiah Greengrass then burst in and began to rummage through the selection of fruit and vegetables which were displayed in boxes on the floor just below the magazine rack.

In a post office-cum-shop that had, moments ago, been a haven of rustic tranquillity, there was now considerable turmoil due to the lack of space while the three of us each tried to avoid the others as we made our selections. It was inevitable we would bump into one another and get in one another's way, but it seemed none of us was willing to stand back to permit a more orderly gathering. It seemed that each of us was in a hurry to complete our purchases.

Standing behind the counter and watching events with a bemused expression on his face, was the owner of the premises, my former sergeant Oscar Blaketon. Towards the end of his police service at Ashfordly, he had expressed a desire to own a small business of this kind, but even so I found it difficult to know what was going through his mind now that he was a postmaster and small-time shop-keeper. It was a complete contrast to his earlier responsibilities as the man in charge of a moderately sized but very busy police station. Now, his busiest day was when the village pensioners came to collect their dues.

Certainly, in a civilian capacity, he had had to curb his capacity for organization and telling others what to do, and I wondered if he felt he should take control of this little incident in his post office-cum-shop. Perhaps he would have shouted for us all to stand back a moment, to allow the first customer – me, in fact – to make his selection, then the second and finally Greengrass. But he didn't; he stood back with a broad smile on his face as each of us jockeyed for position among his tightly packed displays. As I hunted through the cards, I could see him watching us with more than a hint of amusement, and then I found one which appealed to me. It was for my brother-in-law and so I picked it up, found a matching envelope and headed for the counter.

But at that very same instant, so did Greengrass, and the tall, smart stranger. Greengrass was clutching one brown paper-bag full of carrots and another containing mushrooms, while the stranger had a copy of *The Times*, the *Gamekeeper and Country-side*, and *Country Fair*. It was almost inevitable that we all arrived together at the counter – and then I noticed a change of expression on Blaketon's face. In a trice, his bemused look was replaced with one of subservience, and he focused all his attention upon the tall, smart stranger. It was as if Greengrass and I did not exist.

'Yes, sir,' he beamed to the stranger.

'These papers, please, a packet of twenty Players and a bar of fruit and nut,' and the man handed over a pound note.

'Hang on, I was first.' Greengrass pushed closer to the counter and thrust out his hand with the cash.

'You'll have to wait just a second, Claude, while I deal with Mr Mountford.'

'No, it's fine, I can wait,' said the man.

'No, it's time Mr Greengrass learned his manners, Mr Mountford. Now, let me see...' and Blaketon began to tot up the amount owing.

But Claude was not going to be outdone. He slammed his money on the counter before Blaketon, then turned to walk out, saying, 'I'm in a hurry. If it's wrong, you know where to find me. Two pounds of carrots and half a pound of mushrooms.'

'I'm sorry about that, Mr Mountford.' Blaketon seemed keen to apologize to the smart man.

'Think nothing of it,' smiled Mountford. 'It was nothing.'

As the door slammed shut behind the departing Claude, I waited. I was not in a particular hurry and when Mountford had paid, he turned to smile at me, thanked Blaketon and left.

'You know who that is?' I wasn't sure whether Blaketon was making a statement or asking a question.

'No, no idea,' I had to admit.

'Jonathan Mountford, the new magistrate. He lives in Ashfordly, he runs an insurance broking business.'

'Ah, that Mountford!' I had heard the

name. 'But I had no idea he was a magistrate?'

'Then you should know, Nick!' barked Blaketon, more like his old self. 'It is the duty of every local constable to know these things.'

'So how long has he been on the Bench?' I asked.

'Two months, which means I find it very surprising that he is not known to the constables of this area, Nick. Now, if I was in charge at Ashfordly...'

'I've not attended court in that time,' I told him. 'It's these new procedures, evidence being accepted in statement form and all that; we don't get so many court appearances now.'

'That is no excuse. You should know by sight every magistrate who sits in your local petty sessional division. Magistrates are very important local officials. Now, if I was the sergeant at Ashfordly–'

'Can I pay for this card, Oscar? It's my day off and we're taking the children to the beach at Sandsend. I don't want to hang about.'

'I detect a distinct lack of professionalism here, Nick.' He had to have his final say. 'I will talk to Sergeant Craddock about this when I see him; it's time he did something to ensure that all magistrates are known by sight.'

'I agree it would be useful,' I said. 'But I've not seen anything in the newspapers about Mr Mountford's appointment, and nothing on the noticeboard in the police station.'

'Then it is time for action!' said Blaketon, accepting my payment. I left him to his thoughts, went home and wrote out the card, and within half an hour was heading for the beach at Sandsend in our family estate car.

I thought nothing further about Blaketon's comments, but when I returned to duty a couple of days later, Sergeant Craddock hailed me as I entered Ashfordly Police Station.

'Ah, Constable Rhea, just the fellow,' he beamed. 'I believe you have had some kind of confrontation with ex-Sergeant Blaketon, the matter of not recognizing a new magistrate?'

'I was off duty and shopping, Sergeant, just as Mr Mountford was not sitting on the Bench at the time. I would hardly call it a confrontation.'

'Call it what you will, there is no excuse for not recognizing magistrates, PC Rhea.

In light of that experience, therefore, I have discussed the matter with the super-intendent and he has arranged, with the approval and assistance of the magistrates' clerk, for every magistrate to have his or her photograph taken. These will be circulated to all police stations and displayed on all noticeboards throughout the division so that every constable will become very familiar with the appearance of all our local magistrates. I think this is a very positive step forward and an excellent idea, even if it did emanate from Blaketon.'

'Yes, well, I'm sure it will help,' I agreed.

When I left the police station, I must admit I thought Craddock had overreacted to this situation and I felt sure Mr Mount-ford would not have wished to be recog-nized or confronted while going about some small domestic chore – and I wondered if he had recognized me? After all, I had not been in uniform but I was a local constable who regularly patrolled the district.

If I should have recognized him, then likewise, he should have recognized me! Maybe all police officers should have their photographs taken for the same reason? But, as things tend to do within the police service, the idea was implemented within a week or so, albeit not in a very professional way, and eventually Ashfordly Police Station was in receipt of a handful of posters bearing the mugshots of members of the local Bench. It was immediately evident that the pictures had been taken by a police photographer because they were full face, head and shoulders only, in black and white, just like the pictures of criminals which we circulated in our crime bulletins. The full size poster, with the heading 'Do You Recognize These People?' contained photographs of each of the twelve magistrates who served within Ashfordly Petty Sessional Division, and it identified the chairman of the Bench along with our newest member – Jonathan Mountford. He was one of several new magistrates appointed within the county. There was also a picture of the magistrates' clerk. Mr Eldred Wimp. Beneath each picture was the name of the person to whom it referred, but, I noticed, there was no physical description. The photographs did not reveal the height of anyone, nor the colouring of their hair, nor the type of clothing they might be wearing when not in court. But it was a step forward and we exhibited one poster on the noticeboard within the charge room of Ashfordly

Police Station, one on the noticeboard outside for the public to read, one in the cell passage and one in the sergeant's office. The others were distributed to rural beat stations like Aidensfield where I was told to hang one poster in the office so that I might always be aware of the features of these people, and to place one on the noticeboard in my front garden. The latter was for public consumption.

In spite of these efforts, however, the positive identification of people from photographs is never totally reliable. In real life, characters tend to differ considerably from passport-type pictures, a fact borne out by a colleague of mine who was seeking a confidence trickster. My colleague, a detective, called at a seaside boarding house where the con man had supposedly stayed for a couple of days and, being a meticulous police officer, he produced his warrant card to show to the landlady as proof of his own identity. It bore his photograph. She glanced at the photograph, looked him in the eye and said, 'No, I've never seen him.'

Other stories are told of people who recognize characters they have seen on television. Because, for example, a newsreader or weather forecaster appears daily on one's screen, many people recognize him or her – but because those appearances are within the confines of one's own home, a surprisingly large number of viewers believe that the person on the box also recognizes them. I have several friends within the world of TV, and many tell tales of how viewers honestly believe the famous personality is a close personal friend. That arises solely from the fact they appear within the home on such regular occasions. Others see famous people in the street or on holiday, and think I know that person from somewhere, often without realizing who it really is, or where they have previously seen them. They make inane remarks like, 'It is you, isn't it?', or 'It is him, isn't it? Him off the telly?', in the latter case speaking as if the personality is absent.

It follows that the positive identification of criminals is often fraught with danger. If a witness sees a photograph in a newspaper or on television, the image can linger a long time in the memory, and when confronted with the real person, a witness may think, I know I've seen that person somewhere before. In this way, an innocent person could be identified as a criminal fleeing from the scene of a crime. The witness knows he or she has seen that person somewhere (even if it is nothing more than the sight of a paper photograph) and they can easily believe they saw him at the scene of a crime – that kind of thing has happened many times. It has even been known for actors, taking the part of villains, to be 'identified' in the street as someone on the run from the law.

It is with the dangers of identification from photographs in mind that, if identification by a key witness is crucial to a criminal case, the suspect's head and face are covered with a blanket to avoid photographs being taken, or to avoid witnesses seeing them in the flesh and 'identifying' them later. Without a blanket obscuring the suspect, a witness might see the suspect in custody and believe, later in court, that he or she was the suspect observed at the scene of the crime. Memories can play tricks, as most of us know.

It was against this background that I wondered if the system of displaying the photographs of magistrates would really be beneficial. Catching sight of a magistrate driving a car, visiting a pub or a shop, sunbathing, or simply walking down the street differs greatly from seeing one sitting in court or attending to some other kind of judicial matter, like signing summonses or warrants.

Whether or not any of us would recognize the magistrates from their mugshot style photographs was open to question. We could only wait and see.

The first indication that someone was taking notice of those displayed photographs was when the local paper took up the story. It prompted a feature writer to produce a series about people in public service, outlining the work they did on behalf of society in general, and reproducing their photographs beside the articles. Part of the series was an article on the magistracy and so photographs of our local justices of the peace, as magistrates are sometimes called, were reproduced. There was little doubt that my 'confrontation' in Aidensfield post office had led to spin-offs that I could never have anticipated. But it was good to see the work of all these people highlighted in this sympathetic manner.

But all this publicity had an unexpected result.

PC Greg Fortune was a newcomer to the area, having previously served in the northern part of the North Riding, around

Guisborough, Redcar and Loftus. He came to Ashfordly section as a full-time GP car driver. This change meant we would take our turn when Greg was off duty for any reason. He was a keen young constable, anxious to undertake his duties to the best of his ability, and there is little doubt he had promotion in mind. He regarded his GP car duties as just one step on the ladder to promotion, for it was an additional kind of valuable practical experience he could record on his personal file.

The snag with very keen young constables was that they could quickly upset the balance between the more adult-minded and experienced local police and their public – for example, the police of Ashfordly tolerated cars parked without lights, provided they were in the side streets and owned by the residents. They did not rigorously enforce the laws governing late drinking in pubs unless there were complaints, and they closed their eyes to lots of minor infringements of the law, preferring to proffer suitable advice rather than prosecutions. But keen young constables like Greg Fortune soon undo the work of months by sticking tickets on all cars without lights, making pubs close their doors prompt at closing-time, catching people placing street bets, or bets in pubs, especially on the Grand National or The Derby, or prosecuting drivers for speeding at 35 m.p.h through Ashfordly's 30 m.p.h. limit at four o'clock in the morning. Greg never closed his eyes to any minor offences – his eyes were always wide open; for him, there were plenty of offenders to catch.

It was with some trepidation, therefore, that we heard of Greg's transfer to Ashfordly and while we did try to educate him into our way of law enforcement coupled with our own interpretation of 'public service', it seemed Greg preferred to do things his own way – i.e. to enforce the law to the letter, as a means of showing that he knew the law and performed his duties without fear or favour.

It so happened around this time that a confidence trickster was known to be travelling in the north-east of England. His MO was to stay at good-class hotels and leave without paying, often running up bills in local shops, obtaining petrol without paying and even buying a car after producing false details of a bank account.

The man used a variety of aliases, including Jack Mountfield, Joe Monkford, Jim

Mortimer, Jason Monksfield, Justin Montgomery and Julian Montefiore. He was described as about six feet tall with dark, well-cut hair, dark eyes, a fresh complexion, and usually wore smart dark twopiece suits or a blazer and grey flannels with a white shirt and dark tie. He was very well spoken, totally charming and at ease in the most distinguished of company, sometimes producing a gold-plated cigarette case or a wallet bearing his monogram. He seemed able to produce a wad of cash too, and one of his techniques was to charm a lady, somewhat older than himself, into becoming his partner over a dinner – then, on a pretext of becoming romantically attached to her, would trick her into parting with cash. He would say it was for a short-term loan, of course, but such loans were never repaid. Not every woman made a complaint, the embarrassment preventing them from compounding their distress, but some brave ones did inform the police. Whatever the rogue's true name, he was a clever and cunning confidence trickster and he was then being hunted over the length and breadth of Great Britain. Now he'd come north.

All the constables based within Ashfordly

and Brantsford section paid regular visits to hotels and boarding-houses on our patch to warn them against the activities of this smooth character, but it was Greg Fortune who caught him. The fellow had been dining at the Ashfordly Eagle Hotel when Fortune, off duty at the time, recognized him from a photograph which had been circulated. Greg, wasting not a minute, rushed to the table and arrested the suspect, and then marched him unceremoniously, with one arm held behind his back, to Ashfordly Police Station.

Sergeant Craddock was on duty at the time, with Alf Ventress performing office duty. It was Alf who later told me the tale.

'Now then, Greg, who's this you've brought in?' smiled Alf upon seeing Greg and his prisoner at the counter.

'Jason Monksfield alias Jim Mortimer alias Joe Monkford alias dozens of other names, Alf, including Julian Montefiore and Justin Montgomery. The confidence trickster. I arrested him at the Eagle, Sergeant, entertaining a lady.'

'I am not a confidence trickster!' snapped the other. 'I am a well respected business-man!'

At this altercation, Sergeant Craddock

came through from his office and smiled at Greg. 'Well, PC Fortune, it seems you have caught the man we've all been seeking.'

'Yes, Sergeant, at the Eagle Hotel.'

'Now wait a minute!' cried the prisoner. 'You have to listen to me. I've tried to explain to this officer on the way here, but he will not listen. I was about to enjoy a nice evening meal with my mother and this character accuses me of being a confidence trickster. I demand to see my solicitor.'

'All in good time, sir,' beamed Alf Ventress. 'Now, PC Fortune, bring him round here, to this side of the counter and give me the details of the arrest so that we can complete the charge sheet.'

'Well done, PC Fortune,' beamed Craddock. 'It's not often we get a nationally sought-after arrest in Ashfordly. Now, what made you recognize this man?'

'Well, he's been circulated in our crime reports, Sergeant, under his various names.'

'Yes, yes, I know that; we've saturated the district with details of his activities and his many names, but how did you recognize him?'

'From his photograph, Sergeant.'

'And where was that published? I have not seen any photographs of this confidence trickster in any of our police circulations. So far as I understand things, he's always managed to avoid having his photograph taken because he's never been caught.'

'Well, I've seen it somewhere, Sergeant...'

'Of course you have!' snapped the prisoner. 'I am Jonathan Mountford, your new magistrate. My photograph was distributed to all police stations. Look, it's over there on your noticeboard this very minute.'

'Jonathan Mountford, Joe Monkford, Jason Monksfield ... so what's a name?' beamed PC Fortune.

But Sergeant Craddock's face had turned a deep shade of purple as he realized that the man standing before him, under arrest, was none other than the new magistrate. But he recovered almost instantly and, drawing himself to his full height, asked, 'And have you any means of identification, sir?'

'Yes, my driving licence,' and Mountford dug into his pocket, eased out his wallet and then his licence which he passed to Craddock.

'And what was his conduct at the Eagle Hotel, PC Fortune?' Craddock was not going down easily. He was using all his talents as a police officer to extricate himself from what was potentially a serious dilemma.

'He was entertaining a lady much older than himself, Sergeant, one of the MOs used by the suspect.'

'It was my mother, Sergeant, she's still there. You can check if you wish. Now, may I please leave? My dinner will be getting cold...'

'I am not quite sure,' said Sergeant Craddock. 'Your name does bear a marked similarity to the wanted person; you were at the hotel with a woman older than yourself, whom you claim to be your mother ... I am not totally convinced...'

Alf told me that Craddock put on the performance of a lifetime, after which Jonathan Mountford began to wonder whether in fact he would ever be free, but in the end, after calling in a fellow magistrate who lived in Ashfordly who could identify Mountford, the fellow was released without charge.

Mountford, with agreeable charm, was surprisingly calm about his experience and he did not threaten to make an official complaint to the chief constable. He left the police station saying he had learned a lot from his experience and he would be able to put it to good use in his career as a magistrate, particularly when the question of identification arose.

'Sergeant, I'm surprised you didn't recognize him from his photograph,' Alf Ventress said later.

'Now then, PC Ventress, there is no need for that. You didn't recognize him!'

'Well, actually I did,' grinned Alf. 'But I wanted that young upstart of a constable to be taught a lesson.'

'Well, Mountford was utterly charming about it all, PC Ventress, so young Fortune may consider himself very fortunate; his own name has proved his salvation. Mountford could have made an almighty fuss about wrongful arrest, you know.'

'But he didn't, Sarge, fortunately.'

'I wonder why?' beamed Craddock. 'I just wonder why? PC Ventress, what do we really know about our new magistrate? I mean, just consider the facts ... those names...'

I am sure Sergeant Craddock began to make very discreet enquiries into the background of Jonathan Mountford who then, less than six months later, moved his insurance business to a new address in Kent. That meant he had to relinquish his post of magistrate for Ashfordly Petty Sessional Division. I must admit I did wonder why he had decided to move.

If the story of Jonathan Mountford illustrates how one's memory can play tricks so far as visual images are concerned, then so does the tale of John Cranswick. John lived in Aidensfield but worked in Eltering, about seventeen miles away. He was employed in a small factory which produced small metal fittings such as spindles, axles and other parts for objects like radiators, power tools, lawnmowers, engines of various kinds and household utensils. In his late thirties, John was a decent man with a nice wife called Sandra but they had no children.

They lived in a pleasant semi-detached home on the outskirts of Aidensfield, just along the Elsinby Road. John was usually described as a 'very ordinary sort of chap', the kind one would never notice in a crowd. Modestly dressed, often in a T-shirt and jeans when at home, he had a pleasant face, a good head of light brown hair and a slender figure not yet given to middle-age spread. He lived a quiet life, popping into the pub on a Saturday night with his wife for a drink and a snack, and enjoying a game of cricket during the summer. Apart from those two modest interests, he did not take a major part in village affairs, although if there was something like a charity sale for village hall funds he would lend a hand in the arrangements and would often manage one of the stalls, invariably helped by his wife. Sandra also worked; bespectacled and mousy, she was secretary for a solicitor in Ashfordly and managed to run her own second-hand Austin Mini.

The one thing John cherished, however, was his own car. It was a bright red soft top MG Roadster which he maintained in immaculate condition in spite of using it for his daily trip to work. Most week-ends would find John tending his car with loving care, cleaning, polishing, doing minor maintenance jobs and tuning its lively engine. When he was not attending to his car, he and Sandra would use it for long runs into the countryside, sometimes to enjoy a hike across the moors or to visit some of the spectacular houses and castles in the Yorkshire countryside.

If John was meticulous in the care of his car, he was similarly meticulous in his daily routine. For example, he left home at precisely 7.45 every weekday morning for his drive to work.

Although he completed the journey in just under half-an-hour, he allowed himself three-quarters of an hour for the trip in case there were problems, such as a puncture, unexpected diversions and other unknown hazards. This also allowed him ample time to park at work, get his overalls from his locker, clock in and be at his bench precisely at 8.30. John was never late for work.

During my patrols in the area, I would often see his distinctive car heading towards Eltering in the morning or returning in the evening, and one could, quite literally, check one's clock against his daily routine. I quickly realized it was not only I who noticed his precisely timed trip to and from work. The lady who worked in the post office at Briggsby, a large cheerful lady called Bonney Brown, would often mention him whenever I popped in during my rounds. She drove daily from Stovensby to Briggsby and always passed John *en route,* albeit travelling in the opposite direction.

'If I see him before I get to Corner House at the Crampton crossroads, I know I'm late and I've got to get my skates on,' she would laugh. 'He comes along that road every day, regular as clockwork and I know other folks, like me, rely on his timing. I always wave too, and he waves back.'

Other local people would pass similar comments, one lady telling me that she was usually taking her milk bottle in when John passed on his morning trip; one old man would look out for John as he was breakfasting because he liked to see the little red car and the secretary of Maddleskirk primary school said she could rely on seeing John's car just as she was emerging from the sideroad leading from her own cottage.

John's journey to work was so much a part of the weekday routine that existed between Aidensfield and Eltering that few of us in Aidensfield paid much attention to him. Like the sunrise, he was always there but I was reminded of his daily drive when a farmer's wife told me about some annoying thefts.

Because Ashfordly and Brantsford police sections had been amalgamated under the control of Sergeant Craddock, rural constables like me found ourselves patrolling a greater area. On this occasion I was in Slemmington. This lovely village with its gentle river, expansive village green with a maypole, and delightful stone cottages, had formerly been within Brantsford section. Although not far from Aidensfield, I had rarely patrolled it in the past but now it was part of my expanded patch – and PC Jim Collins, the local bobby in Slemmington, would now visit Aidensfield on a more regular basis.

Slemmington lay on a loop of road which had formerly been the main road between Ashfordly and Eltering. A bypass had been constructed to segregate Slemmington from main-road traffic and it now enjoyed a serene and peaceful existence, far from the madding cars. At a point where the old road left the new, there was a farm entrance; this led to Throstle Nest Farm, a thriving concern belonging to Sheila and Harry Kerr. One of the features of this farm entrance was the sturdy oak platform just outside the main gate, for this always bore a selection of produce which passers-by could purchase. Their honesty was assumed and they were asked to place their money in a large stout wooden box which was locked and bolted to a leg of the platform.

Depending upon the season, that platform might bear strawberries, raspberries, plums, apples, potatoes, carrots, cabbages, turnips, lettuce, tomatoes and even fresh eggs or bunches of flowers, all priced and neatly packaged. There was never an attendant at the table. It attracted its regular customers as well as the occasional passer-by; there was a small layby just beyond the farm gate so that cars could pull in and park without becoming a traffic hazard. So far as I knew, the Kerrs had never complained about people failing to pay for their purchases.

Once a month, however, that platform bore a special treat. Sheila Kerr made her own cheese and she produced wonderful round individual cheeses weighing two pounds each. On the first Wednesday of every month, therefore, she displayed a stack of these cheeses on the platform. They were arranged in a tier at the back, twenty-five in total and all stacked like a pyramid. The regulars knew of this wonderful monthly opportunity and such was the popularity of the cheeses that they quickly sold out. Many consumers claimed that Throstle Nest Cheese compared favourably with Wensleydale, and was tastier than Cheddar.

One morning, as I was becoming acquainted with the village and its residents, I decided to visit Throstle Nest. Like all the farmers in this vicinity, they made me most welcome and produced for my enjoyment a mug of creamy coffee, a slice of fruit cake and a whopping piece of Throstle Nest Cheese. I introduced myself and explained our new police patrolling system, then Sheila, a stout middle-aged woman with grey hair and lovely rose-coloured cheeks, said,

'I don't want to bother you, Mr Rhea, because I know PC Collins is on holiday but I thought I'd better mention this.'

'That's why I'm here,' I said.

'Well, somebody's taking my cheeses without paying. Three at a time, Mr Rhea.'

'From the display at your gate?' I wondered, for a moment, if someone was paying surreptitious visits to the farm premises.

'Yes,' she nodded. 'I'm not saying everyone is totally honest, we do lose the odd half-dozen eggs or occasional bag of carrots but I never complain. That's the price we have to pay for putting stuff out unattended by the roadside but most people are very trustworthy. I know how much stuff I put out and what income there should be from its sales, and I know how many cheeses I put out – it's always twenty five two-pounders because I can only produce so much at any one time.'

'And the thief is taking three at a time?'

'Yes, I'm sure he is. Or she is. The price is three shillings and six pence for each cheese, but I put a note out saying buyers can have three for ten shillings. That's a discount of sixpence. When I do my totting up at the end of the day, I've noticed we're ten shillings down some Wednesdays – exactly the price of three cheeses.'

'Have you any idea who might be taking them?' I asked.

'No,' she shook her head. 'The platform can't be seen from the house, but as they've been disappearing for a few weeks now, it's obviously a regular passer-by.'

'It will be almost impossible to catch the thief,' I had to remind her. 'If anyone was waiting nearby, like you or me, they'd either pay or not take the stuff, and even if we did catch someone in possession of three cheeses, he could say he'd paid. It would be impossible to prove otherwise – unless you saw him make off with them. But I will keep an eye open and I will tell my colleagues to do the same. There are a lot of regular passers-by, aren't there?'

'Yes, it's a very busy road nowadays, Mr Rhea,' she agreed.

'Does anyone stand out in particular?'

'Not really,' she said. 'I take the stuff down in my pickup just after eight and it takes a few minutes to set my stall out. I do see folks coming past regularly – there's a school bus, a chap on a motor bike, another one in a red sports car, two young lasses in a blue Mini; they all come past every day as I'm setting up, well every weekday that is, not at weekends, but they never stop, they haven't time; they're going to work I expect. I think it's later in the day when the stuff is stolen. I take it in about five or half-past and collect my takings, but it's not often I'm down there at other times.'

'A whole day unattended? You could change your system,' I suggested. 'Don't put the cheeses on display, just put out a notice there saying they're available from the house.'

'Well, I do get people coming to the house anyway, Mr Rhea, but folks like to look at the displays out there without anybody pressing them to buy. I sell a lot of cheeses that way, and a lot of other produce.'

'The risk is worthwhile then?'

'Oh, yes, I still make a profit, even allowing for losses, but it's so annoying, people being dishonest and stealing stuff I've worked so hard to produce.'

'Right, well thanks for telling me. I'll mention this to our local bobbies and ask them to keep their eyes open when they're along this road, but I do think you should change your system of putting valuable cheeses out. And if you see anyone stop and leave without paying, just get a note of their car number and a personal description, then tell us.'

I left Throstle Nest feeling there was nothing else I could do, other than sit and wait behind a hedge all day in the vain hope I'd catch a sneak cheese thief but I would discuss it with Sergeant Craddock. I had to make sure he was aware of these thefts but, as expected, he decided not to 'crime' the losses.

'We cannot consider this a crime, PC Rhea. After all, there is no proof that the cheeses, or anything else for that matter, have been stolen. How can we prove one person has paid and another has not in those rather casual circumstances? No receipts are issued. Anyone could claim he'd put money in that box. It might be slack bookkeeping by the farmer's wife, too. I've always thought these roadside stalls were a gift to dishonest people and those who place them there do so in the knowledge that a small percentage of stuff is sure to be stolen. That is not to say I agree with theft, I don't, it is always a crime, but for our purposes – official purposes – we need to be sure a crime has been committed. But make a note in the occurrence book. I will instruct our officers to keep our eyes open and make enquiries.'

As I motored home afterwards, I recalled that Sheila Kerr had mentioned a red sports car which passed her gateway every day as she was laying out the produce. Knowing John Cranswick's route and his rigid timetable, I calculated it was probably him on his way to work. I thought I would ask if he had noticed anyone behaving suspiciously around Sheila's stall, either on his way to work or upon his return journey. It was a Saturday morning when I called and found him at work in his garage, with the MG's carburettor on his work bench; he was cleaning it with some petrol and a brush and was up to his elbows in grease with pipes and leads and nuts and bolts all over the place. He looked as if he was thoroughly enjoying himself. I wondered if he could put it all together in time for Monday morning so that his car would get him to work.

'Hello, Mr Rhea,' he smiled. 'Do you want me?'

Just a chat, John,' I said. 'I don't want to interrupt you.'

'I knock off for a coffee about now. Fancy one?'

'I never say no!'

And so we adjourned to the house where John washed his hands in the sink, leaving a black stain all over it much to Sandra's annoyance, then we settled at the table while she organized coffee. And then she produced a plate containing slices of gingerbread – and a partially cut Throstle Nest two-pounder cheese. Gingerbread and cheese are traditional Yorkshire fare, but I began to wonder whether I should accept a piece of that cheese! But, believing John was totally trustworthy and beyond any such suspicion, I accepted a helping.

'Nice cheese,' I smiled as I tasted it. 'Home produced too.'

'I get it from work,' John said. 'One of our workers lives in Slemmington and we can order it from her, direct from the farm. We love it.'

'It's a bit like Wensleydale, soft and creamy.' I chomped away at my piece. 'I believe Mrs Kerr does a good trade in her Throstle Nest cheese.'

'It's very popular. I'm pleased John can get

it from work. Do you know her?' asked Sandra.

'That's why I'm here,' I smiled, and explained about the missing cheeses, along with the casual method of payment. 'I know you go past that way every day, John, and I wondered if you'd seen anyone hanging about her stall, looking suspicious.'

'She's often putting the stuff out when I go past on a morning,' he said. 'I've not seen people stopping to buy it then, but at night, when I come home from work, the stuff is still on display and I have seen people helping themselves at that time. It's a regular stop for some people going home from work but I've no idea whether they're honest enough to always drop the money into her box.'

'Maybe you'd keep an eye open for us? You're one of the few people I know who passes there every day.'

'But I don't,' he smiled. 'Not every day.'

'Oh, I thought you were one of the regular users of that stretch of road?'

'I am, but I vary my route, to stop myself getting bored. Every alternate day I take another route, I go through Thackerston and Stovensby. It's a narrower road but quieter, and it takes me exactly the same time as my other route.'

'Well, according to several people I've talked to, they all say you travel that route every day!'

'The chap in Stovingsby garage says the same thing!' grinned John. 'Sometimes I stop there to get a fill up on the way home, and he always says he could set his clock by me. He told me he watches me go past every morning at three minutes past eight, just after he's opened up.'

'And you don't?'

'Not every morning – I go past his place every alternate morning. I've often thought that if I needed an alibi, I could produce lots of witnesses who would swear they saw me on the road in my little red car when in fact I wasn't there because I was using the other route.'

I traced other people who drove past the entrance to Throstle Nest every day and my colleagues also made enquiries in the locality, but no one had noticed anything untoward so far as stealing the produce was concerned. PC Jim Collins continued the enquiries when he returned from holiday, but we never found any witnesses to the theft of Sheila Kerr's Throstle Nest cheeses. I must admit there were times we wondered if they were really being stolen or whether she was just too lax in her accounting methods.

It would be some six or eight weeks later when I was next in the Slemmington area and I made a point of popping in to see her. I began to explain what we had done, along with the outcome, and she said, 'Oh, don't worry about it, Mr Rhea. Somebody put a brown envelope in the box, it contained three pounds ten in ten-shilling notes. A little note inside said the person was sorry not to have paid for the cheeses they'd taken, as they'd not had any money on them at the time.'

'And did that square the books?' I asked.

'Yes, it did. I told PC Collins, but clearly he's not had time to tell you yet. It only happened last week.'

'So there are no missing cheeses to account for?' I smiled.

'No, everything's in order. But thanks. You know, it might have been your enquiries which prompted the person to pay up. I know that word got around the area that the police were investigating my missing cheeses!'

'All's well that ends well,' I smiled.

As a matter of interest, I visited the garage

at Stovingsby and asked the proprietor, Len Stuart, if a little red, open top MG drove past every morning. And he said it did; he was quite adamant about it, and so was a customer who happened to be filling his tank as I was asking the question.

I did made some enquiries to establish whether or not there was another such car on the road at that time, but there wasn't. So far as anyone knew, John Cranswick's MG was the only car of that description in the district.

And so, according to very reliable and positive eyewitnesses, John Cranswick and his little red MG managed to be in two places at the same time. I often wondered how a court of law or a jury would cope with their conflicting statements.

Chapter 8

When visiting a neighbouring police station, an inspector told me to fetch his desk diary which he kept in a drawer of his desk. I opened the drawer and saw, pinned to the inside, a notice which bore this wording: 'As I sat in the midst of gloom and black despair, I heard a voice, as if from heaven, saying unto me, "Cheer up, things could get worse". So I cheered up, and sure enough, things got worse.'

Three sets of circumstances which happened on my patch reminded me of that doom-laden message and I think it is fair to say that some people do suffer more than others from regular mishaps and constant cruel happenings. For some reason, life does not treat them kindly and usually it is not their fault. They are not careless, stupid or wicked – it is just that life seems to deliver them a regular dose of misfortune and uninvited drama.

In one such case, I remember an old man who seemed unable to avoid setting his house on fire. Not one of his many fires was deliberately started, but it was almost guaranteed that every passing week produced some kind of unwanted blaze in old Joe Matlock's house or garden. His chip pan would catch fire; coals would tumble from his open grate to set the hearth rug ablaze; his bonfire would spread to wooden fences or nearby trees; candles he insisted on using on his bedside table would set fire to the curtains or bedclothes; his pipe had set fire to his jackets and cardigans more times than anyone could remember, and when he tried to strip paint from his front door with a blow lamp, the door caught fire and so did his hair. Most of these blazes were fairly minor, and Joe was able to deal with them himself.

Some, however, were much more serious and I was told that, in the past, three of his homes, two henhouses, three cars and countless garden sheds had been destroyed by Joe's larger and more spectacular accidental fires, in addition to the many hearth rugs, curtains, frying pans, jackets and sets of bedclothes. Although he lived alone and some thought he needed the care of a woman or even a cleaner, none dared spend much time in his house and most certainly, no one would invite him to stay, not even for a cup of tea. The risks were just too great. Everyone felt it would be like living with a roving naked flame which was constantly seeking something to consume. Fortunately, all Joe's fires were quickly discovered by himself, friends and neighbours, and although Joe was given oceans of advice by those living nearby, the basis of which was 'never play with fire', he survived to create many more blazes with each passing year. One villager suggested that when Joe died and was buried, the Fire Brigade should be notified and a fire extinguisher or hose reel should be permanently sited near his grave. Many also pondered the possibility of a fiery destination for his immortal soul while one suggestion was that his gravestone carry a few words from Swinburne's *Hymn to Proserpine,* i.e. 'As a fire shall ye pass', or that instead of declaring the dates of his birth and death, it should record the dates he was ignited and then extinguished.

If that kind of misfortune followed Joe Matlock all the days of his life fortunately without harming anyone else – then it seemed that Derek Barthram was similarly afflicted, although his troubles were directed towards his car.

Derek was a charming young man, full of fun and always cheerful, who worked in an estate agent's office in Ashfordly. In his early twenties, cherubic with blond hair, he was boistrous, very keen on sports like football and cricket, and always active around the village. He would lend a hand to anyone who needed it – he'd help to lift crates of beer into the pub if he was passing, help old folks carry their shopping, light fires for pensioners, clean cars for those less capable than he – and much more besides. Everyone liked Derek. He had a succession of delight-ful girlfriends, none of whom he regarded as potential marriage material; he would take them out for drinks, go dancing or visit the cinema and, if he liked them very much, they could expect an invitation to ride in his car.

At the start of this tale, his pride and joy was a smart blue open top Austin Healey Sprite – his very first car. Although it had been third or fourth hand at the time of his purchase, and some six or seven years old, he cherished the little vehicle as if it was brand new. One bonus was that its sporty image was very eye-catching and highly potent in Aidensfield – there is little doubt it attracted the girls.

During my patrols, however, I discovered that, after the passage of a few months, no one would ride with Derek in his car. At first, I guessed it was because of poor driving standards, although I must admit he always drove carefully and courteously whenever I saw him. To my knowledge, he was never in trouble with the law for any driving offence or carelessness. If his driving skills were not the problem, I wondered if his amorous intentions became rather too lusty once ensconced with a lovely girl in the romantic surrounds of his car?

Many country girls would not tolerate overt lustiness before marriage – so they claimed. But, as I was to learn, that was not a reason either. I did notice that he never took his car to work. He caught the bus from Aidensfield to Ashfordly; his car was reserved for use during his leisure moments, I realized. I thought this might be due to a shortage of parking space near his office, or because it was cheaper to travel by bus – and, of course, he had travelled to work by bus before becoming the proud owner of a car. But that was not the reason.

As I grew to learn more about Derek and his car, I discovered that the little sports car, although looking so attractive and efficient, was most unreliable. For no apparent reason, it would break down at the most inopportune time, such as when he was rushing off to work, or when he had a girl aboard whom he wished to impress, or to whom he wished to present a romantic and efficient image. It was because Derek's car broke down so often that he no longer drove it to work – but he did persist in trying to woo the girls in his blue Sprite.

A sports car which apparently suffered engine trouble in romantic and secluded settings was one thing; one which broke down on the moors in pouring rain was quite another, especially when the soft top would not close properly, or the wheels had sunk up to the axles in mud. Over the months, I came across Derek at various locations around Aidensfield, usually with his head under the bonnet or the wheels jacked up with him lying beneath. I lost count of the number of times I towed him home or gave him a lift to the garage to fix carburettor troubles, electrical faults, ignition failure, brake failure and clutch failure, a jammed accelerator, umpteen punctures, one broken exhaust and even a burst radiator.

I politely suggested he might have unwittingly bought a grossly defective vehicle but he assured me he'd had it examined by a friend who was a mechanic and also by Bernie Scripps at Aidensfield garage, both of whom had pronounced there was nothing wrong with the car. They had examined it before Derek had committed himself to buying it, and again after he'd experienced a barrage of troubles, and for a vehicle of its age, they had pronounced it in very good condition. Those of us who knew of Derek and his troubles began to wonder if he, or the car, was jinxed.

Then one dark Friday night, with the rain cascading in torrents, I came across Derek's car parked on the side of the road on the moors between Aidensfield and Briggsby. The hood was raised and I could see a lone, dim outline of a figure sitting forlornly inside. I was on duty and cosy in the warmth of my police van, so I eased to a halt behind the Sprite upon which Derek's door opened and he galloped towards me with a coat over his head.

'Oh, it's you, Mr Rhea, thank goodness! I thought no one was going to stop.'

'Jump in.' I leaned across and opened the passenger door at which he dived in and shook his coat outside before closing the door.

'More trouble?' I asked as he settled down.

'Pretty serious by the sound of it,' he groaned. 'Big end I think, or something important's broken. Valve problems maybe. Whatever it is, it made one hell of a noise and I came to a standstill. I managed to freewheel it backwards off the road, but I wasn't going to walk home in this lot. Thanks for stopping.'

'So where do you want to go? The garage? Or home? Or the pub to drown your sorrows?' I asked, pulling away from the verge.

'I think it's time I got rid of it,' he said seriously. 'It's been nothing but a load of trouble since I bought it. So take me home, Mr Rhea, if you don't mind. I don't want to spend any more on it, I'll advertise it as scrap. Mebbe Claude Jeremiah Greengrass will take it off my hands. On second thoughts, though, I might just get dried out and pop down to the pub for a pint. Claude is sure to be there. I'll talk to him about it.'

Claude did buy the little car from Derek at a knockdown price, and a few days later I saw it undergoing repairs in Bernie

Scripps's garage. I popped in for a chat.

'Are you trying to make a good car out of that heap?' I laughed.

'It's not in bad fettle.' Bernie's mournful voice didn't sound too encouraging. 'It's got a broken drive shaft but that can happen to anybody.'

'Derek's had a load of trouble with this car,' I added.

'I know, I've had it in here time and time again, Nick, but most of the things could happen to anybody, like punctures and so on. It's not a bad car. Claude got a bargain here, and when I've got it back on the road, it should be all right for months. It's a good little car, Nick; it's just that Derek's been unlucky with it.'

'So Claude's going to sell it, is he?'

'That's his idea, yes. It's a bit small for his purposes. I'll sell it for him, for a bit of commission, of course. I'll stick it on my forecourt once I've got it ready. It'll sell easily enough.'

A week later, I spotted Derek Barthram in another handsome vehicle, this time an immaculate Sunbeam Alpine, a two-seater sports car with an open top. It was a warm tan colour and it looked splendid. As I was patrolling towards Aidensfield post office, he drew it to a halt at my side.

'How's this, Mr Rhea?' Derek beamed. 'This'll get the girls and just you listen to this engine...'

As he revved it, the engine sounded beautiful, smooth and powerful and so I looked around the car, admiring its overall design, the upholstery, fascia and white-walled tyres.

'Very nice,' I complimented him. 'Very nice indeed. Let's hope you have more luck with this one.'

'One lady owner – and I've had it checked over by the AA,' he said. 'They said it is faultless. And my mate who's the mechanic, he gave it a going-over and said the same. No rust, no wrong engine noises, no dodgy rattles in the gear box, clutch in good condition, new exhaust only last month, good tyres, no play on the steering, serviced just before I bought it with new plugs, points and brake linings, not using excessive oil ... it's like new, Mr Rhea.'

I must admit it did look as good as new and it had clearly had a very careful owner for it was in pristine condition. I wished him well and watched him drive along the street and out of my sight with a cheery wave. Meanwhile, at the other end of

Aidensfield main street, his former Austin Healey Sprite was displayed for sale on Bernie's forecourt.

Bernie had given it a thorough check and had pronounced it fit and roadworthy, and the following Saturday, a young woman called Sally Kirkman bought it. She had it inspected by her father, the AA, two mechanics and a friend, all of whom said the little car to be as near perfect as was possible for a car of that age. Bernie had done a very good job on the vehicle and she purred away with her long blonde hair flying in the afternoon sunshine.

Derek's Sunbeam, however, broke down the first time he decided to drive a girl to the pictures in Ashfordly. The fuel pipe had fractured close to the petrol tank and he had come to a halt on double yellow lines close to a bus stop. A traffic warden did not believe the story of his breakdown, gave him a ticket and threatened to have it towed away if it was not moved within a couple of hours. He said it was causing an obstruction. This was the prelude to a period of more dramas and breakdowns. I lost count of the number of punctures suffered by Derek in this car; there were umpteen occasions when the electrical and ignition systems failed; the top hose burst on two occasions to drench the engine in hot water; the exhaust cracked in two after he'd negotiated a water splash; one of the rear springs collapsed; the steering became defective and his handbrake cable snapped.

'They're just teething troubles, you expect something to go wrong with a car of this age,' he told me with a show of confidence and bravery one Saturday morning as he was filling up at Bernie's. 'I can soon get things fixed and it'll be like new once I've ironed out all the problems. I mean, Mr Rhea, the bodywork is in very good condition, not a hint of rust.'

Then, one late October night, with a gale blowing across the moors and roaring through the woods and forests, and with torrential rain filling the becks and racing down the roads, I was on a late patrol in my Mini-van when I saw the familiar figure of Derek Barthram trudging through the rain. He wore a raincoat which seemed totally ineffective against the ferocity of the storm and so, as I had done on so many occasions, I stopped to offer him a lift. It was about 10.30 and very dark.

'Trouble, Derek?' I asked as he settled into the passenger seat, smoothing down his windswept hair and trying to make himself comfortable.

'I've run out of petrol at Devil's Hole.' He sounded dejected. 'I've been to Ashfordly, to see a pal of mine from work, and I think somebody's nicked some petrol while I was parked in Highdale Road. I remember there was a smell of petrol around the car when I returned to it, but in this storm, I didn't hang around to check. When I set off, I thought the needle was showing empty but I knew I'd filled it up yesterday so I thought the gauge must be faulty...'

'I'll run you to Bernie's,' I offered. 'He'll fill a can for you.'

'No, he'll be closed at this time of night. Mr Rhea, I don't want to trouble him now. I can do it tomorrow, the car will be safe enough – at least nobody can drive it away!'

'So where is it?' I asked.

'In the dip at Devil's Hole,' he said. 'It's off the road. I managed to run it on to that patch of spare ground at the bottom of that cliff; you know, where fishermen sometimes park.'

'I know it,' I said. 'It'll be sheltered there, that overhanging rock and those trees will keep some of the rain off it. I'm on patrol until two o'clock,' I added. 'I'll keep an eye on it until then.'

And so I took Derek home. As the night hours passed, so the storm intensified and while I motored through the villages upon my beat, I found myself clearing from the roads several large branches which had been smashed from overhead trees. There were broken tiles on the roads too, blown from nearby houses, then I spotted a henhouse whose roof had been blown off and a greenhouse, several of whose panels had been smashed. Conscious of my own safety, I patrolled as best I could to check that no one was injured, but most people had the sense to remain indoors. Tomorrow, though, there would be a need for everyone to check their roofs for missing or broken tiles, and their property for other signs of storm damage.

And then, not long after midnight, with the storm losing none of its ferocity, I received a radio call from Ashfordly. It was Sergeant Craddock who had probably decided to remain on duty due to the awful weather conditions.

'Ah, PC Rhea,' he said. 'I am glad I was able to raise you; I thought you may be out of contact in these gales. Is the storm affecting your beat?'

'It is, Sergeant.' And I briefed him on the extent of the storm so far as I could.

'Well, the reason for my call is that a motorist has reported a tree down on your beat, in Devil's Hole. It has apparently crashed on to a sports car which was parked beneath it, but my informant assures me there is no one in the car. Can you check it out? Trace the owner and make sure no one is lying there injured.'

'Will co, Sergeant,' I said. 'I think the car belongs to a man on my beat, Derek Barthram. He reported it to me not long ago, he'd run out of petrol so he had to leave it there.'

'Very careless of him,' he said.

'It was stolen, Sergeant,' I said, tongue in cheek. 'The petrol, I mean, while he was parked in Ashfordly.'

'Well, the crime has not been reported to us, I would have known if it had,' he snapped. 'But check it as soon as you can, then you'd better go and break the news to the owner. And the owner of the tree will have to make arrangements to have it moved with the minimum of delay, it is partially blocking the road.'

Driving down the narrow, twisting lane into Devil's Hole, I could see the wreck of

Derek's precious Sunbeam; not only had a tree crashed upon it, so had a portion of the overhanging rock. The stocky oak had been clinging to the cliff face, its roots some-where deep within the fissures of the rocks, and the effect of the storm had sent the oak crashing to the ground, taking a large chunk of rock with it. The tree had fallen length-ways upon the car, crushing it from boot to bonnet, and the top of the tree reached almost to the centre of the carriageway. I was not sure of the safety of the remaining rock face, but I had to make sure no one was in the car – after all, a passer-by, such as a wandering tramp, might have climbed in for shelter during the storm. Extremely wary of the dangers, I approached the remains of the car – it had been flattened beneath the weight of the oak and the rock, the combination of which had reduced it to a heap of splayed wheels, crushed metal and torn leather. In the lights of my own vehicle, and aided by a powerful torch, I searched for any sign of a person in the car, but there was none. I was most relieved that Derek had not remained with his car, and once I was sure it had been empty at the time of the tree's collapse, I placed some traffic cones around the edge of this patch of ground to prevent anyone else parking, and from the remaining equipment carried in my van, positioned a pair of flashing amber lights on the road to warn approaching traffic of the partial blockage.

After radioing Ashfordly Control to provide a situation report, it was time to break the news to Derek. It was approaching one o'clock when I arrived at his parents' home and although I thought the news could have waited until dawn, I felt duty bound to inform him immediately. Derek answered my knock. When, in his pyjamas, he opened the door and saw me, the expression on his face anticipated my news.

'It's the car, isn't it?' he said before I could utter a word.

'Sorry, Derek.' I felt genuinely sorry for the lad as I told him of the tragedy.

'I nearly slept in it,' he spoke softly. 'I nearly thought there was no point going home and leaving it, but I'm glad I did.'

'You were very lucky,' I said, hoping to soften the blow a little.

'Yes, I was, wasn't I? That's the first bit of real luck I've had in years. Maybe things will get better now?' He produced a smile which suggested he would welcome a change of fortune. 'Thanks for telling me. I'll have to arrange to get it shifted, won't I?'

'The owner of the tree will have to get his tree shifted first,' I said. 'I think that land belongs to Ashfordly Estate. I'll tell them tomorrow morning, then you can have words with the estate manager, he might even arrange to have your car taken to a garage. He should take some responsibility for your damage.'

'Better still, they could take it to a scrap yard. It'll be beyond repair, won't it?'

'It is,' I agreed. 'It's a complete write-off. Ring your insurance company in the morning.'

'Right, and it's such a good job no one was hurt, eh?'

'Yes, a very good job.' I was impressed by the way he coped with the news but after all the bad luck he'd experienced with his cars, he'd had lots of practice dealing with misfortune. I left him to return to his bed and set about completing my patrol, hoping there would be no further serious incidents during the night. Apart from what might be described as normal storm damage, there were no fatalities, no more serious incidents and very little flooding.

The next time I saw Derek, I thought he

was very philosophical about the fate of his Sunbeam and there is no doubt he felt extremely lucky that he'd not been injured, but it was sometime before he decided to get another car. Having made that decision, he wanted to tell me.

'I'm collecting it tomorrow,' he told me as he emerged from the post office one Saturday morning. 'A nice Hillman Minx, a saloon.'

'Not a sports car this time?' I asked.

'No, I've had enough of open top cars, what with rain and storms and breakdowns and falling trees and punctures...'

'Well, I hope you have better luck with this one.' I was sincere in my good wishes for him. 'Is it new?'

'No, it's second-hand but in excellent condition. I got a cheque from the insurance company for the Sunbeam and I thought a saloon was a good idea. I can carry more passengers, it'll be more comfortable and, more important, cheaper to insure.'

And so Derek Barthram, bought himself a handsome blue and cream two-tone Hillman Minx. I saw him cruising along the village from time to time, sometimes alone and sometimes with a girl as a passenger, then eventually I realized he was using it for work. It would be about two months later when I had a chat with him.

'How's the car?' I asked. 'Any trouble with this one?'

'Not a bit!' he smiled. 'I think it was sports cars that were jinxed when I bought them. Maybe someone somewhere, was trying to tell me something? Trying to say that sports cars and me just do not mix!'

'Maybe,' I agreed and I smiled as he left me to join a lovely brunette who was waiting in the passenger seat.

Another person who suffered a bewildering run of bad luck was Paul Hammond, a forty-five-year-old former flight lieutenant in the RAF.

A pleasant and affable character, Paul was married with a grown-up family. He had served at Fighter Command stations in Yorkshire and when the time came for him to retire, he decided to fulfil a dream – he'd always wanted to establish a small restaurant and tea-room, and his time in the North Riding had revealed the charms of rural north Yorkshire. With tourism an expanding industry, he'd recognized the potential of establishing his business in Ashfordly. With the security of his savings, his RAF pension and his retirement gratuity, he'd managed to raise the capital necessary to commence his enterprise. I understood the banks had helped him by granting substantial loans to transform the interior of the building he had purchased so that it met the standards required for such a business. He called it Yorkshire Fare. It was an old and very spacious house which overlooked Ashfordly market place, a prime setting to catch both passing customers and residents. His initial idea was to live in a top floor flat above the restaurant until his venture was well established, and then find another home somewhere not too far away. He could then let the living accommodation, either to a chef or to holidaymakers. The banks had also agreed to provide enough capital to equip his restaurant with the latest cooking facilities, refrigerators and freezers, wine cellar and essential furnishings like tables, chairs, crockery and utensils. It was with immense pleasure and pride, therefore, that Paul Hammond's dream became a reality. He opened Yorkshire Fare with a flourish of good will and lots of advertising, and then all he had to do was work hard to make it profitable.

Official police interest in such an

establishment was minimal – Paul had a restaurant licence which allowed him to sell drinks to customers taking table meals but our professional involvement with Yorkshire Fare was slight indeed. Many of us did support him by using the premises for celebrations such as birthdays and anniversaries, and if anyone asked us to recommend an establishment for business entertainment or simply for a really good private meal, then we would suggest Yorkshire Fare. We knew it would please anyone who patronized it. The food was good, the surroundings very pleasant and the prices reasonable. It was not surprising, therefore, that the restaurant and accompanying tea-room were always busy.

Clearly, the business was successful and after some two and a half years, Paul and his wife, June, decided it was time to move out of the flat and into a cottage. They found Linnet Cottage which is just across the bridge as one enters Ashfordly from the Briggsby direction, and they bought it. Only 200 yards from the restaurant, it required a good deal of modernization, but as it had been sold at a very reasonable price, Paul and June were prepared to regard it as an additional investment by spending some of their savings upon it. Once the cottage was fully modernized, they would move in; the plan was for the chef to occupy the flat above the restaurant or, if that did not work, then it could be let, either on a long term to a tenant, or in the short term to holiday-makers. Business was booming and Mr and Mrs Paul Hammond soon established themselves as leading business people in Ashfordly. They were pleasant, well regarded, efficient and helpful; they supported local charities, helped to sponsor the town's football team and allowed their premises to be used once a year, free of charge, to host a fund-raising event for cancer research.

And then, quite inexplicably, things began to go wrong. Most of us realized that few of the subsequent problems were the fault of either Paul or June, but the overall effect was dramatic. The first, and probably the worst, was an outbreak of food poisoning. A party of a hundred and ten diners had attended a high profile event at Yorkshire Fare to raise money to buy a new sports field in Ashfordly, and of them, forty two had later been affected with some kind of stomach cramps and dreadful diarrhoea. Although no one had died, several were extremely ill and required hospital treatment. The cause had been traced to a consignment of chicken used in the preparation of the dinner at Yorkshire Fare and the subsequent investigation led to rumours that the kitchens of the restaurant were unhygienic. Trade slumped dramatically – customers stayed away and parties cancelled their bookings and then, to add to the problems, the chef was found to have been dealing in stolen wines – he had been stealing from the cellar of Yorkshire Fare and selling them to his contacts in Middlesbrough. His dishonesty was discovered during the enquiries into the source of the food poisoning and he was eventually sentenced to three months' imprisonment. Paul and June's attempts to rebuild their business after those two highly publicized setbacks were decidedly difficult; no one would apply for the position of chef in an establishment with a reputation for unhygenic working conditions.

It mattered not that the source of the poisoning was later found to be the supplier of the chicken – the damage to Yorkshire Fare, fuelled by unsupported rumours, had already been done. It was later revealed that two other premises, one in Eltering and the other in Brantsford, had also being affected, albeit in a less spectacular manner, but in spite of that, the hitherto highly regarded Yorkshire Fare was now labelled with a very unhealthy reputation.

Paul and June's income fell alarmingly at the very time they needed substantial funds to finance their expansion schemes. But worse was to follow.

At the time of these disasters, they had already committed themselves to improvement work at Linnet Cottage. Builders had been commissioned and the work was too far advanced for it to be halted. To make the cottage habitable, it had to be completed – and the builders had to be paid. In the light of their reduced income, Paul and June decided to let Linnet Cottage as a holiday home when the improvements were finished, and they would continue to live in the flat above the restaurant, at least on a short-term basis. As no one suitable had yet applied for the post of chef, the cooking would be done by June, and much of the routine administration and drudgery would rest upon Paul's shoulders. This meant they would function with as few paid staff as possible. And so they buckled down to make the best of what was becoming more of a joint liability than an asset. Their efforts were not made easier when another up-market restaurant opened in Ashfordly. It offered a menu of wonderful food prepared by a cordon-bleu chef. Diners flocked to the new restaurant as they abandoned Yorkshire Fare, but in spite of their difficulties, June and Paul continued to work hard, producing very good, inexpensive meals and within three months trade began to recover, chiefly because it was summer when hordes of tourists came to visit Ashfordly. As they came from afar, they knew nothing of the dramas surrounding Yorkshire Fare and consequently patronized the restaurant and tea-room, even if many local people continued to go elsewhere. But business did improve; there were no more outbreaks of food poisoning; essential work continued at Linnet Cottage and after a traumatic few months, Paul and June began to smile again.

Then PC Phil Bellamy was patrolling past Yorkshire Fare at three o'clock one morning in late summer when he noticed water pouring from beneath the front door. After weeks of hot, dry weather, there had been some heavy thunderstorms, with localized flooding in places, but this water was cascading out of the house and down the steps, then flowing into the street where it vanished down a drain. The place was locked but he knew Paul and June slept in the flat and so he began his attempts to rouse them by banging on the restaurant door. He failed – then hit on the idea of radioing Control and asking them to telephone the couple; surely they would have a bedside telephone in the flat? His scheme worked; lights appeared and Paul's head appeared from his bedroom window.

'What is it?' he shouted down to Phil Bellamy.

'You've got a burst,' Phil shouted back. 'A pipe or something, water's pouring out of the door!'

Minutes later, Paul was opening the door to admit Bellamy and they were confronted by a dreadful sight – the whole of the restaurant floor was standing in two or three inches of water, beneath which lay the carpet. Fortunately, the water had found an escape route through the gap beneath the front door – but in the meantime, it had spread into the kitchens, the tea-room, the toilets and the bar area. Carpets and rugs were ruined, some furniture had suffered and, of course, the wooden floors beneath the carpets would also be saturated.

'Turn it off at the main!' Bellamy shouted as June now joined them to gaze in horror at the mess.

'That's no good, it's coming up through the floor!' Paul had cried.

And so it was. It was not coming from the mains supply. It was later discovered that, with a hot and very dry summer, the clay base beneath the old house had dried out and an underground stream, fed by a spring, had taken a new route. Normally flowing deep underground beneath some adjoining gardens to emerge in Ashfordly Beck just off the market place, its new route had encountered a blockage and so it had overflowed along the line of least resistance – to well up beneath the old premises which were now Yorkshire Fare. The flow had to go somewhere – and so it had seeped up through the floorboards of the restaurant to spread around the ground floor until it had found an exit route.

At the sight, June broke down in tears while Paul realized the full horror of this new situation. This kind of flow could not be turned off with the twist of a tap handle – there was no way of stopping the water.

The whole floor would have to be

removed and efforts made to install pipes which would direct the flow into some suitable drainage system – a truly mammoth operation. And so Yorkshire Fare was compelled to close down, at least during extensive and expensive operations among the very foundations of the old house. I didn't know whether Paul and June's insurance company accepted any liability for the repairs and redirection of the spring water, but they continued to live in the flat as the recovery work began.

But, with no income from the restaurant or tea-rooms, and with huge borrowings to service, we all knew they faced ruin. They did, however, have a very small return from Linnet Cottage – that had been renovated to the point where it could be let to holiday-makers and so the first customers were already enjoying the pretty cottage. The income, however, was just sufficient to cover the full cost of renovating the cottage – Paul and June's savings had paid for much of the improvement, but further borrowings had been arranged to cater for the extra work which had been found necessary. To sustain the income necessary to fund the cottage repayments and upkeep, it needed to be let for some forty-five weeks out of every fifty-two. By that autumn, there was no change in the situation – Yorkshire Fare was closed as the ground floor of the old house was gutted with experts trying to cope with the non-stop flow of spring water, although it had, by now, been directed into a custom-built drainpipe. That was a temporary measure, however, for the now unstoppable flow needed to be directed completely away from the foundations of the house.

The inevitable outcome was that Paul and June decided to sell the restaurant and tea-room once the repair work was complete, and they also decided to sell Linnet Cottage. They wanted to make a completely new start somewhere else. I became aware of this decision when I asked about vacancies for a friend and his wife who wished to visit the North York Moors for a couple of weeks over Christmas.

'Sorry, Nick,' Paul said. 'We're giving up. Everything's against us, we've tried and the gods have decided Yorkshire Fare must close. I'm putting Linnet Cottage on the market too. We've bookings until the end of December – I've a landscape artist coming to stay for a month and he's due out on January 3rd. He wants to capture some winter moorland scenes. When he's gone,

I'll remove the furniture, then the place can be sold at it stands. By my calculations, we should just about cover our costs, it'll mean starting from scratch all over again.'

'I'm sorry,' I said. 'You've certainly had a run of bad luck.'

'I always thought I was a lucky guy,' he smiled ruefully. 'A good career in the RAF, a loving and supportive wife, the chance to do this in my early retirement ... but, as I said, the gods are against me. So we've decided to sell up and then we'll make up our minds about what to do next.'

In the weeks that followed, work progressed on the foundations of the old house and expert contractors managed to divert the stream through a system of pipes and tunnels. The building was allowed to thoroughly dry out; a new floor was installed and, in time, the former restaurant was given a new life, this time as a large old house. Paul and June felt it would sell more easily as a spacious old house.

As I patrolled Ashfordly from time to time that autumn, I did see people coming and going from Linnet Cottage, and then the landscape artist moved in for the month of December. His name was David Boyce; he was an elderly gentleman with a flowing white beard, long white hair and a rather hunched figure which was probably the result of bending over easels throughout his working life. His work was very popular and I looked forward to the outcome of his few weeks in Linnet Cottage. I knew he was due to leave on 3 January, by which time I had learned that Paul and June had hoped to dispose of Yorkshire Fare's premises with a view to establishing a brand-new bed-and-breakfast business at St Ives in Cornwall.

I did feel sorry for Paul and June, but had to admire them for the calm and courageous way they coped with their problems. I saw them before they left Ashfordly. A few days before Christmas, they came into the police station while I was on office duty.

Paul said, 'Ah, Nick, just the fellow. Linnet Cottage. I'm told you keep a register of unoccupied properties, so you can keep an eye on them?'

'We do,' I confirmed. 'We check them several times daily.'

'Well, we leave Ashfordly tomorrow, but Mr Boyce, the artist, will occupy Linnet Cottage until 3 January – that's a Friday. He's alone, and he'll leave the keys with Manor Estate Agents upon departure. Then the following Tuesday, 7 January, a removal van will arrive to take all our furniture from the cottage. They'll take it to our new home in Cornwall. Once that's done, the cottage will be put on the market with vacant possession.'

'A completely fresh start?' I did feel sorry for them but both seemed confident and anxious to cope with the future.

'A whole new beginning, yes. Manor Estate Agents will handle everything for us at this end. I just wonder if the police would keep an eye on Linnet Cottage until it's sold? I'll leave our new address and phone number.'

'No problem,' I assured them. 'I'll put the details in our Unoccupied Property Register. I hope things work out better now you've made this decision.'

'I don't think it could have been worse!' Paul sounded rueful. 'Everything bad that could have happened did happen – apart from plagues and thunderbolts! But at least we gave it a try. Nothing ventured, and all that! And, I must say, it was good while it lasted. We made some nice friends and both of us learned a lot about running a catering business. We can put our experiences to good use.'

'I'm sorry you're parting with Linnet

Cottage,' I said.

'So are we,' added June wistfully.

'It's such a good-looking house,' I went on. 'A wonderful introduction to Ashfordly as you drive over that bridge on the way in. If I was in the housing market, I'd like to buy it myself, it's always appealed to me.'

'That's why it caught my eye,' June smiled. 'Every time we drove down the hill into Ashfordly, it always seemed to be welcoming us. It sits so beautifully as the town opens up behind it. I often said to Paul I'd like to live there, but it didn't quite work out. We nearly made it though! Maybe one day we'll retire and come back. Who knows?'

'Well, I hope so. But rest assured we'll keep an eye on Linnet Cottage for you, I hope you sell it quickly.'

'I'm confident of that,' he said. 'There's a big demand for traditional cottages of that kind. It's almost certain we've sold our big house too, there's a lot of keen interest. I've been talking to an hotel chain but it'll remain on the market until the deal's been finalized. It'll make a nice private hotel, so fingers crossed!'

And so they left, with me shaking their hands and wishing them every success for the future. Several potential buyers continued to be shown around the former premises of Yorkshire Fare and by New Year, the group of small hotels was showing more than a passing interest, albeit with a proviso that the water course situation was examined with great care. Apparently satisfied, the group then put in a bid, having explored the possibility of being granted the necessary planning permission for change of use. In the meantime, David Boyce could often be seen heading back to Linnet Cottage after a day's painting on the moors. Following the Christmas holidays, I was driving past Linnet Cottage on Saturday, 4 January, and noticed the curtains were closed.

According to what Paul had told me, David Boyce would have left the previous day; it meant the Hammonds' links with Ashfordly were finally over because the cottage would now be put on the open market. We would keep an eye on it until it was sold – we'd check the doors and windows to ensure no one had broken in – although burglaries would be unlikely once the furnishings had been removed but squatters were becoming something of a social problem in places.

In spite of all that, there was further

tragedy for the unfortunate Paul and June Hammond.

I was on duty in the GP car on Monday, 6 January, and, between 6 a.m. and 10 a.m., was performing an early morning patrol of the entire sub-division. Just before 8.30 a.m. I halted in Ashfordly market place so that I could undertake a short foot patrol while the morning traffic was building up. Almost as I climbed out of the van, I heard an almighty crash somewhere to my right. Almost immediately, I could hear frantic and alarmed shouts, so I dashed to the car, leapt inside, started it and rushed away towards the source of the noise. If there was an emergency, I'd need the car's radio. As I rounded the corner of the main street, I saw carnage. I pulled up on the footpath, blue light flashing, and rushed out.

A heavy lorry, laden with timber, was embedded in the wall of Linnet Cottage, with its cab almost buried in the house and its trailer partially overturned and blocking the entire road. Part of its enormous load had shifted and there were ominous hissing noises coming from the vehicle, plus a smell of escaping diesel fuel. A man was nearby, frantic with anxiety, and when he saw me, he ran over to my car shouting, 'It ran away, down the hill. It just flew across that bridge and just missed me ... you must do something, the driver's trapped in his cab...'

Without wasting a second, I radioed Control.

'Ten nine, ten nine, ten nine.' I realized I was shouting the emergency code, and then I added my own identity. 'Major vehicle crash in Ashfordly; location, Ashfordly Bridge. An HGV with a load of timber aboard has crashed into a cottage and demolished the front wall, driver believed trapped. The cottage is empty. Am at the scene with the GP car and investigating. Assistance from emergency services requested. Imminent risk of fire. Ambulance and doctor needed, with heavy lifting gear. Over.'

I knew my call would be enough to galvanize my colleagues into immediate action. My next task was to establish whether there were any casualties, and if so, the extent of their injuries, along with any likelihood of further danger from fire, any further movement of the stricken vehicle or falling masonry. I could not ignore the fact that one or more pedestrians might have been trapped too – the footpath leading past the cottage was busy at that time of day.

My immediate thought was for the driver and when I battled my way through the tumble of masonry and smashed woodwork, I reached the cab. The driver was behind his wheel, apparently unconscious, but I could hear him moaning. The entire front of his vehicle was crushed. His door had sprung open due to the impact and I could see that his legs were trapped among the pedals by his ankles and feet – he'd need painkillers and ultra-careful treatment. But how long could he remain here? The smell of fuel was dreadful and choking, and the lorry continued to emit those worrying hissing sounds as I fought my way around the front of cab. I was now deep inside the house, coughing my way through floating dust and finding my way around debris and broken furniture as I checked to see if the driver was accompanied.

But the passenger side, not so badly damaged as the driver's, showed the driver was alone – then I realized that, in the absence of a wall to the front of the house, the roof of the cab was supporting the beams of the floor of the bedroom above. If we dragged the lorry from this position, the whole upper floor, or certainly a large proportion of it, would collapse. We were in for a very delicate and difficult recovery of both man and vehicle.

If there is one thing that police officers learn in such circumstances, it is never to take anything for granted. My first duty was to ascertain the number of casualties and I thought I had done that – we had one lorry driver who needed emergency treatment – and then my training took over and I knew I must search the house too. I had assumed it was empty, but it might not have been. I must not make that kind of assumption. Someone might have moved in – even Paul or June – and I knew I must make a swift search, just to be sure. I knew, of course, that the emergency services would have been summoned, and equally, I realized the upper floor was unstable but it is a police officer's duty to save life. And so, shouting at the driver that help was on the way, and hoping my voice would penetrate his unconscious or partially conscious state, I began to search the house. There was no one in this room – or what was left of it – and so I looked in the kitchen, the tiny dining-room and the downstairs toilet. All empty. The staircase, at the rear of the house, seemed to have escaped damage, so I began to climb very warily, shouting a warning of my approach, but no one answered. I checked the bathroom and the rear bedroom, both of which appeared to have escaped damage.

Then I opened the door which led into the front bedroom, the one overlooking the street. It was the one whose floor was now supported by the roof of the lorry's cab, and as I eased open the door, I could see that daylight had flooded the room because part of the outer wall was missing, as was the window.

But there was someone in the bed! And the bed was lying at an angle now because the floor was partially sunk and the edge of the bed was resting against an inner wall.

'Hello!' I shouted at the figure. No reply.

I shouted again, many times, without any response and so, fearing the worst, I stepped gingerly on to that sloping floor. I knew the cab would support my extra weight. As I approached the bed, I realized the occupant was the artist, David Boyce. His white beard and hair was so easily recognizable. But when I touched him, in the hope of rousing him, I knew he was dead. Stone dead. His body was cold and I could smell death. He had been dead a long time.

Then I was aware of Sergeant Craddock

standing behind me.

'A problem, PC Rhea?' he asked.

'There's a dead man in that bed, Sergeant, I think he's been dead a long time. I believe it's the artist, David Boyce; he was renting this cottage from the Hammonds.'

'So,' he said. 'We've a big task ahead of us, have we not? A dead man, not killed by this accident we believe, and hopefully not murdered or the victim of suicide; we have a nasty traffic accident out there with a potential fatality and a fire risk, and we have a house in a dangerous condition.'

'It was going to be put on the market this week,' I told him.

'Well, I cannot see it will reach the market for some time. But come along, we've got to get out of here, we have a lot of work to do,' he said. 'This place is dangerous, too dangerous to linger.'

And so we left to meet the emergency services and to plan our operation, albeit pondering whether to move the dead body first. But life is more important than death; the lorry driver was our first priority and already, the ambulance was outside, the doctor had arrived, heavy lifting gear was *en route*, and we could begin our rescue operation.

'We need to inform the owners of the house, PC Rhea, the Hammonds I believe?'

'Yes, Sergeant, they've moved to St Ives. We have their address and phone number on file.'

'And who's going to break the news to them?' he asked, looking at me with his steady gaze.

Chapter 9

One of the minor but very important duties of the police is to administer reports of lost and found property. Much of this is fairly mundane because people have a tendency to lose or mislay ordinary things like umbrellas, handbags, walking sticks, house or car keys and similar personal belongings. By reporting the loss to the local police, there is always a faint chance their treasured item will be recovered, as members of the public are surprisingly honest when they find things. They will endeavour to have the property restored to the loser either by reporting the discovery to the police or to some other suitable agency in which the thing was found, such as shops, taxis, bus and train companies or hotels.

The police, however, do not make a search for such lost items – they merely record them and rely on the honesty of finders to bring the matter to their notice – although if the missing item is particularly dangerous or noteworthy for some other reason, then a search might be made, accompanied by any necessary publicity. Such dangerous items might include drugs, firearms, ammunition, explosives, surgical instruments, swords and daggers, and anything else which might cause death or injury in inexperienced hands. The police never cease to be astonished at what the public can lose – one driver reported losing his bus; it hadn't been stolen, he'd simply forgotten where he had parked it. A doctor lost his bag of equipment and medicines. He'd placed it on his car roof while he unlocked the door, removed his overcoat, then climbed in to drive off with the bag still on the roof. It was never found, neither was a large clock inadvertently left unattended at a bus stop.

Reports of property found in public places, however, require much more care and attention. If someone reports finding an object, there is always the possibility it might be the proceeds of crime, something thrown away or hidden by a criminal. If the object is not recorded as stolen – or is not subjected to the laws of treasure trove or shipwrecks – then it is entered into the Found Property Register.

At this stage, a corresponding search is made in the Lost Property files to see if a match can be made. If the object has not been reported lost, then, under normal circumstances, the police will ask the finder to retain it. If it is not claimed within three months, it becomes the property of the finder although the original loser always has a claim of right over it. This simple system means that busy police stations are not cluttered with mountains of found objects such as umbrellas, handbags, wallets with no name inside, cameras, boots and shoes, walking sticks, car hubcabs, pedal cycles, items of clothing such as coats and hats, watches, money in the form of cash or notes and more bizarre items. In my time on the beat at Strensford, items of found property included an entire cooked salmon, a wedding cake, a pair of corduroy trousers, a set of false teeth, a lawnmower, a car seat, several unexploded bombs, an artificial leg, a box of five dozen eggs, a piano, a roulette wheel and a one-legged hen.

Clearly, if the object found was of particular interest or danger, or if it was perishable, then special arrangements were made. The wedding cake, cooked salmon and eggs to which I have just referred were not quickly claimed, and so, without waiting for the three months to elapse, they were sent to the town's hospital whilst they were still edible.

There were special procedures for dealing with things like valuable oil paintings and other works of art, unexploded bombs, personal documents such as cheques, wills and passports, rifles, shotguns and pistols, jemmies, government documents, confidential files, postal orders or pawn tickets. We sent the one-legged hen to a friendly poultry keeper but we never did find the owner of the artificial leg (to fit a human, not a hen). The piano had been accidentally left on the street during the removal of some household goods. Its owner was traced. We felt sure there were some interesting stories to account for the other unusual objects which found their way into our records.

It was with these general procedures in mind that I had to deal with a fascinating discovery in an outbuilding behind Aidensfield post office. The occasion was Bob-a-Job Week when youngsters in the local troop of scouts undertook a fund-raising exercise by offering to perform small tasks for payment. The original idea was to pay the scouts a shilling (a bob) for doing something like sweeping one's back yard, cleaning the car, weeding the garden, cutting the lawn, polishing one's shoes, washing up, walking the dog or some other small but useful chore. Most people were prepared to pay more than a shilling (5p in decimalized money), provided the work was done well, and the scouts were welcomed by the villagers each time they undertook this special week's work.

During a Bob-a-Job Week, I was in the post office one Monday morning, buying stamps and chatting to ex-Sergeant Oscar Blaketon, when a couple of eager scouts walked in.

Aged around thirteen or fourteen, they were Aidensfield lads and were dressed in their uniforms, looking most efficient. Blaketon broke off our chat to address them.

'Now then, lads,' he smiled. 'Bob-a-job Week is it?'

'Yes Mr Blaketon,' responded their spokes-scout. 'Is there anything you want doing?'

'There is,' he said. 'I've been keeping this job especially for you and if it's properly done, there'll be five bob each. That's ten bob in total – and there could be more if it takes a very long time and if you do a really good job.'

Their eyes lit up at the prospect of such riches – a job which generated ten bob or more was not to be ignored and so they agreed.

'I've a shed behind the shop,' he told them. 'It's full of junk and it needs cleaning out. A lot of it can be burnt – I'll show you where I want it so that I can make a bonfire – and some can be taken away in a wheelbarrow, and I'll show you where that goes. The whole place needs clearing out, so how about it?'

'Yes, we'd like that.'

So Oscar excused himself and led them through the rear of the shop. 'Come and see this, Nick,' he invited me. 'You'll never believe what the previous owner left behind.'

Together, therefore, we trooped into the spacious garden at the rear of the post office where he led us to a row of three brick-built sheds, each with a stout wooden door. I was quite surprised at the spaciousness of his rear garden, but it matched many of the others in this village – long narrow strips of garden were a local feature.

The first shed contained his gardening tools and equipment, the middle one was a workshop complete with bench and tiers of wood-working and metal-working tools, but the third was full of what appeared to be lengths of timber and assorted junk such as rolls of wire, broken chairs, an old kitchen cabinet and much more besides. He spent a few minutes explaining to the scouts how to sort out the rubbish into separate piles, and what would then happen to each pile, and the lads set to work with enthusiasm. At that stage, I left to continue my patrol.

Later that same day, around 4.30, I returned to the post office to post some official mail and Blaketon hailed me.

'Ah, Nick,' he said, emerging from the shop. 'A word, if I may.'

He led me inside, and indicated an elegant statue which stood on the counter. It was slightly more than a foot high and had been carved from what looked like a piece of solid oak. It depicted a smooth-faced man wearing clerical robes and a mitre; he was carrying a bishop's crozier and was standing on a small plinth. There was no colouring on the statue, it being plain wood, but it was in remarkably good condition.

'What do you make of that?' he beamed.

'A nice piece of work,' I said. 'Beautifully carved. Who is it?'

'You tell me,' he said. 'I've no idea who it

is supposed to be, how old it is or who carved it. Those scouts found it in my shed.'

'Did they really? Is it valuable?' was my next question.

'I don't know that either,' he said. 'To be honest, I don't know what to do about it.'

'You're not reporting it to me as found property, are you?' I put to him.

'No, that's not necessary, it was found on my private premises. I've had words with my solicitor, the one I used to purchase these buildings, and he says the statue belongs to me. I bought the post office and shop, and all the outbuildings, lock, stock and barrel, as they say. But, to be honest, Nick, I don't feel I've any true claim to it.'

'Well, if it was part of the property which you purchased, and you acquired it in good faith, I can't see there's a problem.'

'There isn't a problem, not in law I mean. It's mine, Nick, I know that, but I don't feel happy about keeping it. I'd like to know more about it for one thing, its history, who it depicts, who carved it and so on, and whether it is very valuable or important. And I think those scouts should have some claim too; after all, if it hadn't been for them, it would never have been found.'

'If it hadn't been for *you*, you mean. If it

hadn't been for you, it would never have been found. You set the necessary work in motion, you paid them to clean out the shed. Have you made any enquiries about it?'

'Yes, the first thing I did was to ring Joe Steel, the chap who ran this post office before I bought it. He said he'd never cleared any rubbish from that shed; it was all there before he bought the place, and that was over twenty years ago. I did try to ring the man who'd had the place before Joe, but he's dead, so I talked to his son. He said the shed was full of rubbish when he lived here, and that was before the war. That rubbish has been there for years and years, no one's ever cleared it away.'

'So how old is the statue?' I asked.

'Who knows?' And he spread his hands wide in a gesture of hopelessness. 'I was hoping you might shed a little light on it, you've been here longer than me and I know you've delved into the history of Aidensfield. Have any famous sculptors lived here, for example? Or was any famous bishop born here? Is the statue associated with Aidensfield in any way, or is it nothing more than an anonymous carving?'

'I can't think of anything useful to tell you,

311

Oscar, but I'll do a spot of research. How about you? Will you be trying to find out more?'

'I'm going to take it to Ashfordly Museum of Rural Life, they have an art expert who might help. And I have spoken to the parents of those two scouts, to tell them I'm trying to find out more. I don't want them to think I'm keeping this all to myself, if it turns out to be valuable or important, I mean.'

'It's very honest and generous of you,' I said. 'But right, I'll bear it in mind, and if I hear anything, I'll be in touch.'

I did examine my various local history books without finding any reference to famous clergymen who may have lived or been born in Aidensfield, and I did not discover any references to famous artists or sculptors, nor even unknown sculptors, who had worked in the village. Some four or five days later, I returned to the post office to buy more stamps and asked Blaketon how his own enquiries had progressed.

'Not very well,' he admitted. 'The art expert at the museum specializes in oils and watercolours of British landscapes, so she wasn't much help, but I have discovered the wood is bog oak, probably fifteenth century or earlier.'

'Does that mean the statue's as old as that?' I asked. I noted the statue was still on display on his counter.

'Not necessarily. In fact, I showed it to a woodcarver I know, and he reckons it is much more modern. A lot of woodworkers have, over the years, been able to get their hands on ancient pieces of oak, from derelict castles, farm buildings, houses and so on, and he thinks that is the source of the wood. He's sure it is a piece of oak, matured in a bog centuries ago, and used in some local building. He thinks the marks left by the carver's tools are quite modern, though, not medieval or anything like that. He reckons it might be no more than a hundred years old, if that.'

'And that's it?'

'So far, yes. Oh, and the art expert felt that the clothing and crozier indicated a bishop or even a saint. She reminded me of all those northern saints, those associated with Holy Island, Whitby and Lastingham. She thinks it might be one of those, and it might have been commissioned for a church.'

'You've had a word with Father Simon, have you?'

'He's not been in here since those lads

found it, Nick, but I intend having a word with him, that's why I keep it on the counter. Or the vicar might know?'

'They're likely to know of any association between Aidensfield and any of those old saints, Father Simon especially, or another monk from Maddleskirk Abbey,' I said. 'If I see any of them, I'll ask them to pop in and have a look at your statue.'

It was the following day when I spotted Father Simon, the monk who was also Catholic parish priest of Aidensfield. He was visiting members of his flock.

'Father Simon,' I hailed him. 'I'm pleased I caught you. Have you been in the post office recently?'

'No,' he looked puzzled. 'Should I have been in?'

I laughed. 'No, but Mr Blaketon has discovered a statue in his outbuildings or rather some scouts have – it's a wooden one, carved out of old oak, and it seems to depict a saint or a bishop. He's trying to find out something about it, I wondered if you might help by having a look at it?'

'Yes, of course. Now?'

'No time like the present. He's open,' I smiled.

'Then you come with me.' And so we

walked to the post office, with the monk asking after my family and chatting about my work. Once inside, he had a short discussion with Blaketon who outlined his enquiries to date, then Father Simon picked up the statue and began to examine it closely in the light of the doorway.

'It's St Aidan,' he said with confidence. 'Not the St Aidan who was also known as St Medoc. That Aidan studied under St David in Wales, but his later work was chiefly in Ireland around Ferns in County Wexford. But the statue is not that Aidan. This is our St Aidan, a local saint. He was actually born in Ireland but worked chiefly in the north-east of England; he established a monastery on Lindisfarne and he was a bishop. He is very much a saint of the north-east of England, Mr Blaketon, and this is an image of him. There is no doubt about that.'

'Can you be so sure?' puzzled Blaketon.

'The few images of him, in art, tend to show his emblem, which is a stag. If you look carefully at that plinth, there is the faint image of a stag on the side. The person who carved this clearly knew what he was doing; it would be added as a means of identifying the saint, although the sculptor has not left his own mark or initials.'

315

'Great! And its age?' asked Blaketon.

'It is very hard to say, I'd guess not very old, Mr Blaketon. Last century perhaps. I doubt if it is medieval, and I don't think it has any great commercial value. It is a very handsome piece of work, however, a well-crafted piece of carving and one which would grace any church.'

'Is Aidensfield named after St Aidan?' asked Blaketon.

'It is, even if the name Aiden or Aidan is spelt slightly differently,' smiled Father Simon. 'Aidan was a Catholic of course, and you'll note that Aidensfield Catholic Church is named in his honour; he is our patron saint.'

'Then I think your church is the right place for this statue,' said Blaketon. 'I'm not at all happy claiming it as mine, so what better resting place than St Aidan's own church?'

And so that is what happened. An ornate shelf was erected on the wall to the left of the altar in St Aidan's Church in Aidensfield, and the statue now occupies it, matching one of the Virgin Mary to the right. There is a small plaque to show how it was discovered by the two scouts and donated by Oscar Blaketon. We never did

316

discover who carved it nor did we establish its age, but St Aidan looks exactly right in his new and more comfortable setting.

Although it is not the duty of the police to seek items of lost property, unless there are very special circumstances, there are times one wishes one could do something to help troubled losers. This is especially so when the missing item is a treasured personal belonging of some kind, not necessarily an object of great financial value. Such a case occurred in Aidensfield when Mrs Connie Hobson lost a necklace.

Connie was a dear old lady, well into her eighties, and she lived in an estate cottage at the east end of Aidensfield. It was tucked behind a row of stone-built houses and access was by a narrow alley between two of those houses. It was impossible to reach Connie's cottage by car but, as she had never owned one, that limitation did not appear to worry her. Stoutly built and sometimes short of breath, she had been a widow for almost twenty years. Her husband, Jack, had worked for Crampton Estate who were owners of her cottage, and she received a tiny pension from them, in addition to having her cottage rent-free for life. Connie was very active for her age and cared for herself. Her two daughters lived away from the village, one in Eltering and the other in Scarborough, but they visited their mother whenever possible.

Connie seldom left Aidensfield, unless one or other of her daughters came to visit her at weekends when they would take her for a drive. About once every six or eight weeks, she would take the bus into Ashfordly to do a little shopping but apart from that, her life was spent in and around Aidensfield.

In spite of her stocky build, she did like walking and every day she could be seen striding along one of the many footpaths which formed a network around the village. Sometimes she would take a neighbour's retriever for a walk, sometimes she'd be accompanied by a child or two, and sometimes she'd walk with anyone using the same route. Affable and friendly, she could always make friends, even with complete strangers. Everyone felt it was her daily walk which kept her so healthy and fit, even if she often seemed short of breath.

Then one Saturday morning, I saw her coming along the path towards my office door and went out to meet her.

'Hello, Connie.' I must admit I was surprised to see her. 'Something wrong?'

I opened the door and showed her inside, offering her a chair. She flopped on to it and after regaining her breath, said, 'I've been to the post office, Mr Rhea, and Mr Blaketon said I should come and see you.'

'You've a problem?' I asked.

'Not a real problem, Mr Rhea. I've lost a necklace, you see. I think it must have been during one of my walks. I went to see if Mr Blaketon would put a notice in his shop window and he said he would, then he said I should inform you. He said somebody might have handed it in.'

'Right,' I said. 'Well, they've not handed it to me, but I can make an entry and search Ashfordly records, just in case someone's reported it there. And if someone does hand it in, we'll know where it's come from. So when did you lose it?'

'That's the trouble, I'm not sure. I wear it all the time, it's never off except when I have a bath and wash my hair. I had it last Friday, a week ago that is. I remember because I took it off to have my bath. Friday night is bath night, you see, and I always put it on the bathroom window sill while I'm bathing.'

'Right,' I said. 'So it's disappeared since then?'

'Well, when I had my bath last night, it wasn't round my neck, you see. I went to take it off and it wasn't there.'

'And you'll have searched the house? And the clothing you wore during the week?'

'I have, Mr Rhea, several times. I've been through everything with a fine toothcomb. Dustbin, laundry basket, airing cupboard, wardrobe, drawers, kitchen cabinet, down the side of my chair, the lot. I think I must have lost it during one of my walks, maybe the chain broke, or the clasp wasn't fastened properly.'

'Is it valuable?' I asked.

'It means a lot to me,' I could see her eyes growing moist at this stage. 'It's always been in the family, you see, for as long as anyone can recall. I can remember my granny wearing it, then my mother, then it came to me. She said it had to be handed down to us through the female side; it had been her granny's, and her great-granny's before that and so on. I don't really know how old it is.'

'And would you have any idea of its value?' I persisted.

'Not a clue!' she smiled. 'That's never entered my head. I've never had reason to worry about that because I'll never sell it; it will go to my eldest daughter.'

'Right, well, first, I'll take down a description.'

She explained that the chain was solid silver and it bore a locket also fashioned from solid silver. She thought it was Jacobean but could not be sure, saying the locket was oval shaped with a silver back and a convex glass at the front. The back could be unfastened with a tiny clasp. This allowed a small object to be placed inside, such as a tiny photograph, or as the Victorians liked to do, a lock of hair from a loved one or some other small token of remembrance. The edges of the locket were decorated with swirls of silver and the top bore a silver coat-of-arms in miniature. It bore a tiny shield adorned with two greyhounds and a hare, and it contained a tiny dark-green gemstone, probably an emerald. She'd never had the necklace valued or examined by a jeweller and was not very sure of its true value or origins. The locket, she said, was about an inch-and-a-half high by an inch wide at the widest point. When I asked if she had a photograph of it, she shook her head, and she also told me it was not insured.

'I can't afford that sort of insurance, Mr Rhea. I did think of offering a reward for its return, but can't really afford it. I mean, if I offered a pound reward, who'd be interested? I'm sure my necklace is worth more than that – maybe if someone has found it, they will try to sell it in the antique shops?'

'That's always a risk if a dishonest person finds it,' I had to remind her. 'Anyway, I will make the necessary records in our files and if it does turn up, we'll be in touch – and if you happen to come across it, you will tell me, won't you? If you lost it during one of your walks, you might just find it again.'

'I'll never stop looking,' she said, her eyes still rather moist.

'And I will pass word around the village,' I said. 'I'm sure that if an Aidensfield person found it, they would be honest enough to hand it in.'

'Oh, I do hope so,' she sniffed.

'I'm sure most of them will see the notice in the post office and it might be an idea to put posters on the parish notice board and anywhere else people are likely to read them. If they know you've lost it, they'll keep their eyes open, I'm sure.'

'I'll do as you say, Mr Rhea, I am quite good at writing notices. It will give me something to do – and I will scour every inch of ground on those walks of mine.'

In the following days, I did my best to make everyone in the village aware of Connie's loss and I had discussions with ex-Sergeant Blaketon about it, but we had to admit that, with the passing of time without any sign of the locket, the chances of its recovery began to grow ever more slender. One problem was the sheer size and nature of the area in which it might have been lost – the surrounds of Aidensfield were covered with woods, fields, hedges, moorland and pasture and the network of paths, covering several square miles, wound and twisted their way through that landscape, often descending rocky routes or passing through marshes. I'm sure Connie had not ventured upon the entire length of every one of them, but even if she managed to retrace all her many walks, her locket could have fallen into the undergrowth or a crevice where it may remain hidden for ever from her eyes and from the eyes of casual passers-by. It began to seem that only a stroke of sheer luck would lead to its recovery.

A couple of weeks later, I received notice that a treasure hunt would pass through Aidensfield on a forthcoming Friday evening, between 6 p.m. and 8 p.m. Such outings were very popular at the time. Not really falling into the category of motor rallies, they involved people travelling in cars who had to work out a route presented to them in cryptic form, and then keep to that route and identify points along the way. They searched for things like dates on buildings, names of houses, fixtures like trees or bridges bearing numbers and a host of other static objects. The idea was to avoid scoring penalty points during the run, the penalties being awarded for late or early timekeeping, exceeding the mileage, taking short cuts, not recording the required objects *en route* and so forth. They were good fun, even if over-enthusiastic participants sometimes annoyed villagers by their exuberant behaviour. After all, having twenty or thirty carloads of people stopping to stare at the name on one's gatepost can be a little embarrassing, especially if one is trying to relax in the front garden at the time.

However, out of thin air, this inspired me to consider the idea of having a local treasure hunt, the object of which was to find Connie's locket. If we obtained a map of the paths around the village, found static points close to each one and arranged a competition so that every path was covered by a crowd of eager youngsters seeking the 'hidden treasure' Connie's necklace – while also looking for those checkpoints, like the Gospel Oak, the Aidensfield Cross, Elsinby Aidensfield Foss, the Hermitage and so on, then it might succeed. I went to talk it over with Oscar Blaketon.

'Well, I can't see any legal objection,' he assured me. 'Mind, we don't want to finish up with lost children or missing grand-parents, and we don't want people breaking their legs or suffering other injuries, and we'd need some kind of check-point system.'

'You make it all sound very formal!' I laughed.

'You can't be too careful these days. But it's not a bad idea, Nick. I would imagine some sort of stimulus would be needed too, a reward of some sort for the winner. He or she can't keep the necklace, that belongs to Connie, (that's assuming we are going to trace it) so we might have to consider a small entrance fee and share it between, say, the person who finds the locket and a charity of Connie's choice.'

'And we need someone to compile the entry sheets for the competitors,' I said. 'Someone who can produce cryptic clues so that a route can be followed. Someone with a very good knowledge of the area. Someone who can cover all those paths in such a way that even the most basic of simpletons doesn't get lost. And, before the event, every one of those paths would have to be checked to make sure it doesn't differ from the information given on our sheets.'

'And suppose the necklace is not found after all that?' he smiled knowingly.

'Well, we would have a penalty-points system, like a motorized treasure hunt, penalties being awarded for failing to visit the check points *en route* – we'd need wardens at all those points to sign competitors' sheets – and the person with the least penalties could be the winner. There could be penalties for getting back to base too early or too late – we could set a time limit. But the overall winner, irrespective of points, must be the person who finds the necklace; if the necklace is not found, then the person with the least penalty points would be the winner. It could all be a bit of lively fun.'

'In spite of my initial caution, I think the secret of this event is not to make it too serious,' Blaketon advised me. 'We could make it too difficult and too serious. It does need to be a bit of fun, with people going along those paths armed with rakes and sickles to clear the undergrowth, or even taking magnets and bloodhounds. Does silver respond to a magnet, Nick? That's the sort of thing you need to be thinking about.'

'I agree – and I think the man to help with the paperwork is Clarence Baldwin, our local historian; he knows every inch of the village and its environs, and he's a good artist.'

'Well, it's your idea, Nick,' Blaketon said. 'It could work. You need to have words with Clarence to see if your idea is viable and then, if it is, we'll go for it. I'll help in any way I can. Poor old Connie is very upset at losing that necklace. It would be lovely if we could find it for her. Even if we don't, she could present the prize to the winner.'

After lots of discussion between myself, Blaketon and Clarence Baldwin, we did feel the idea was viable and so, with Connie's approval, the grand locket hunt got under way. So that entire families could take part if they wished, we selected a Sunday after-noon and when the WI heard about the event, its members said they would arrange teas in the village hall at a small cost.

There'd be a raffle, too.

We decided the event would start and finish in the village hall, with a maximum of two hours' trekking and searching for each person involved in the hunt. Clarence had realized it was impossible for every hunter to explore all the paths around the village within the time available, and so, when compiling his competition sheets, he produced four choices – Routes A, B, C and D, as he called them. Stewards would be positioned around the walks to act as check-points and safeguards. Each competitor could select his or her own route; there was an entry fee of half-a-crown per person out of which expenses would be met and a prize or prizes would be awarded. Any residue would go to the village hall maintenance fund.

The build-up to the Great Locket Hunt, coupled with Connie's pleading notices around the village, promoted a good deal of interest and on the day, there was a wonderful turn-out. The Aidensfield Scout Troop provided a team of lads in uniform; the cricket team did likewise; both churches sent their choirs along; the parish council added ten pounds to the prize money, and the darts team from the pub appeared in the disguise of Robin Hood and his Merry Men. The most touching compliment was that Connie, at 82 and still breathless, appeared at the start and paid her half-crown entry fee – she refused a free trip! She was accompanied by the retriever she often took for walks, saying, 'Goldie's owner can't make it, she's an old lady you know.'

And so, at two o'clock that Sunday afternoon, the hunt got underway with teams of eagle-eyed hunters taking different paths as they sought Connie's necklace and locket.

Some were armed with metal detectors, others had sickles and pruning shears, several had long sticks and torches while Connie herself went along more as an observer than a hunter – after all, she'd already searched every one of those paths without success. The result was that the pathways, woods and moors around Aidensfield that afternoon were full of the sounds of people thrashing the undergrowth, over-turning rocks, shouting to team members, hurrying to check points and scattering startled pheasants. Each knew they must return to the village hall by no later than four o'clock where their entry sheets would be scrutinized and their penalty points totalled as they discussed their outing over cakes and tea. Blaketon, who'd been appointed chief judge, was in charge of the final checking procedures and it was Connie who approached him, rather shamefaced, as the competitors began to return.

'A lovely event, Connie,' boomed Blaketon. 'Wonderful turn-out.'

'Yes, Mr Blaketon,' she smiled. 'But it is all rather embarrassing.'

'Really? And why is that?' he asked.

'Well, I have found my locket,' she told him, producing it from the pocket of her cardigan. 'Or rather, Goldie found it.'

'Goldie?'

'My neighbour's retriever, the dog I take for walks. She started scratching under a bramble bush, down by the stepping stones, and there was my locket, Mr Blaketon ... covered in soil and dirt, but otherwise all right. A link in the necklace had broken, you see,' and she passed it to him for examination.

'Well, I think this is wonderful, Connie,' he said. 'You have found your own necklace.'

'Well, I've been past that place time and time again without finding it, and I suppose if I hadn't had Goldie with me, I might not have come across it ... she found it. I wonder if she smelt it?'

330

'Well, you'll get first prize–'

'Oh, no, I couldn't.' She shook her head vigorously. 'No, I couldn't, Mr Blaketon. I've got my necklace, that's all I want. Give the prize to the person with the least number of penalty points. I think that's only fair, don't you?'

The winner of the fifteen-pound prize was a twelve-year-old boy scout and there was enough cash for a second prize of five pounds. That was won by a lady pensioner. The happiness and community spirit generated by that treasure hunt produced calls for it to become an annual event. We could not arrange for a suitable piece of personal property to be lost, however, although, under conditions of the utmost secrecy, we could conceal a locket and then persuade people to hunt for it. With funds generated by that first event, therefore, we bought a small silver locket, a replica of the one owned by Connie which, throughout the year, would be on display in the village hall before being 'lost', once a year, some-where outside the village. And we'd all enjoy looking for it. From the proceeds of that first event, we purchased a chrome cup which we called The Constance Hobson Cup and thus the hunt for Connie's necklace became an annual event. In time, it became known as the Aidensfield Locket Walk and remains popular with residents and visitors alike.

The publishers hope that this book has given you enjoyable reading. Large Print Books are especially designed to be as easy to see and hold as possible. If you wish a complete list of our books please ask at your local library or write directly to:

Magna Large Print Books
Magna House, Long Preston,
Skipton, North Yorkshire.
BD23 4ND

This Large Print Book, for people
who cannot read normal print,
is published under the auspices of

THE ULVERSCROFT FOUNDATION

... we hope you have enjoyed this book.
Please think for a moment about those
who have worse eyesight than you ...
and are unable to even read or enjoy
Large Print without great difficulty.

You can help them by sending a
donation, large or small, to:

**The Ulverscroft Foundation,
1, The Green, Bradgate Road,
Anstey, Leicestershire, LE7 7FU,
England.**
or request a copy of our brochure for
more details.

The Foundation will use all donations
to assist those people who are visually
impaired and need special attention
with medical research, diagnosis
and treatment.

Thank you very much for your help.